KANAE MINATO

Confessions

Translated by Stephen Snyder

MULHOLLAND
BOOKS

HODDER

Originally published in Japan as *Kokuhaku* by
Futabasha Publishers Ltd., Toyko, 2008

English translation rights arranged by Futabasha Publishers Ltd.
through Japan UNI Agency, Inc., Toyko

First published in Great Britain in 2014 by Mulholland Books
An imprint of Hodder & Stoughton
An Hachette UK company

I

A CIP catalogue record for this title is available from the British Library

Paperback ISBN 978 1 444 73245 0
eBook ISBN 978 1 444 73246 7

Printed and bound by Clays Ltd, St Ives plc

Hodder & Stoughton policy is to use papers that are natural, renewable
and recyclable products and made from wood grown in sustainable forests.
The logging and manufacturing processes are expected to conform
to the environmental regulations of the country of origin.

Hodder & Stoughton Ltd
338 Euston Road
London NW1 3BH

www.hodder.co.uk

CONFESSIONS

CHAPTER ONE

The Saint

Once you finish your milk, please put the carton back in the box. Make sure you return it to the space with your number on it and then get back to your desk. It looks like everyone is just about done. Since today is the last day of the school year, we will also be marking the end of "Milk Time." Thanks to all of you for participating. I also heard some of you wondering whether the program would be continuing next year, but I can tell you now that it won't. This year, we were designated as a model middle school for the Health Ministry's campaign to promote dairy products. We were asked to have each of you drink a carton of milk every day, and now we're looking forward to the annual school physicals in April to see whether your height and bone mass come in above the national averages.

Yes, I suppose you could say that we've been using you as guinea pigs, and I'm sure this year wasn't very pleasant for those of you who are lactose intolerant or who simply don't like milk. But the school was randomly selected for the program, and each classroom was supplied with the daily milk cartons and the box to hold them, with cubbyholes for your carton to identify each of you by seat number; and it's true that we've kept track of who drank the milk and who didn't. But why should you be making faces now when you were drinking the milk happily enough a few minutes ago? What's wrong with being asked to drink a little milk every day? You're about to enter puberty. Your bodies will be growing and changing, and you know drinking milk helps build strong bones. But how many of you actually drink it at home? And the calcium is good for more than just your bones; you need it for the proper development of your nervous system. Low levels of calcium can make you nervous and jumpy.

It's not just your bodies that are growing and changing. I know what you've been up to. I hear the stories. You, Mr. Watanabe, you grew up in a family that owns an electronics shop, and I know you've figured out how to remove most of the pixilation on adult videos. You've been passing them along to the other boys. You're growing up. Your minds are changing as quickly as your bodies. I know that wasn't the best example, but what I mean is, you're entering what we sometimes call the "rebellious period." It's a time when boys and girls tend to be touchy, to be hurt or offended by the least little thing, and when they're easily influenced by their environment. You'll begin to imitate everyone and everything around you as you try to figure out who you are. If you're honest, I suspect many of you will recognize these changes in yourselves already. You've just seen a good example: Up until a few moments ago most of you thought of your free milk as a benefit. But now that I've told you it was an experiment, your feelings about the milk have suddenly changed. Am I right?

Still, there's nothing too odd about that—it's human nature to change your mind, and not just in puberty. In fact, the teachers have been saying that your class is actually a good bit calmer and better behaved than the usual group. Maybe we have the milk to thank for that.

But I have something more important I wanted to tell you today. I wanted you to know that I'll be retiring at the end of the month. No, I'm not moving to a new school, I'm retiring as a teacher. Which means that you're the last students I'll ever teach, and I'll remember you for as long as I live.

Settle down now. I appreciate your response—especially those of you who actually sound as though you're sorry to hear I'm leaving—what? Am I resigning because of what happened? Yes, I suppose so, and I'd like to take some time today to talk to you about that.

Now that I'm retiring, I've been thinking again about what it's meant to me to be a teacher.

I didn't enter this profession for any of the usual reasons—because I myself had a wonderful teacher who changed my life or anything like that. I suppose you could say I became a teacher simply because I grew up in a very poor family. From the time I was little, my parents told me they could never afford to send me to college—and that it would have been a waste to send a girl anyway—but I suppose that made me want to go all the more. I loved school and I was a good student. When the time came, I received a scholarship—perhaps because I was so poor—and enrolled at the national university in my hometown. I studied science, my favorite subject, and I started teaching at a cram school even before I graduated. Now I know you all complain about cram school, having to go right home from the regular school day to hurry through supper and run off to more classes that last late into the evening. But I've always thought you were incredibly lucky to have parents who cared enough to give you that extra opportunity.

At any rate, when I reached my senior year I decided to forgo graduate school—which might have been my first choice—and get a job as a teacher. I liked the fact that it was a secure career with a stable income, but there was an even bigger factor: The terms of my scholarship required me to repay the tuition money if I did not become a teacher. So without so much as a second thought, I took the test to obtain my license. Now I know this may cause some of you to question my motives for becoming a teacher, but I can assure you I have always tried to do the very best job I could. Lots of people fritter away their lives complaining that they were never able to find their true calling. But the truth is that most of us probably don't even have one. So what's wrong, then, with deciding on the thing that's right in front of you and doing it wholeheartedly? That's what I did, and I have no regrets.

Now, some of you may be wondering why I chose to teach middle school rather than high school. I guess you could say that I wanted to be on the "front lines," so to speak. I wanted to teach students who were still in the middle of their compulsory education. High school students have the option of quitting, so their attention can be divided. I wanted to work with students who were still completely committed to their education, who had no other choice—that was as close to a true calling as I could find. It may be hard to believe, but there was a time when I was passionate about this work.

Mr. Tanaka and Mr. Ogawa—there's nothing particularly funny about that part of my story.

I became a teacher in 1998, and my first position—on-the-job training, really—was at M Middle School. I was there three years and then took a leave of absence for a year before coming here to S Middle School. I found I enjoyed being away from the bigger cities in the prefecture, and this has been a pleasant, relaxed place to work. This is my fourth year here, so I've worked as a teacher for only seven years total.

I know you've been curious about M Middle School. Masayoshi Sakuranomi teaches there, and you've probably seen him on TV recently.... Please settle down, everyone. Is he *that* famous? Do I know him? Well, we worked together for three years, so I suppose you could say I do, but in those days he wasn't such a celebrity. They've made him out to be a super-teacher, and he's in the news so often that I suspect you know more about him than I do.

What's that? You don't know the story, Mr. Maekawa? Don't you watch TV? All right, I'll tell you. Sakuranomi was the leader of a gang when he was in middle school, and when he was a sophomore in high school he assaulted a teacher. He was expelled and left the country, and for the next few years he apparently wandered around the world doing all sorts of dangerous things and getting into trouble. He witnessed war and other violent conflicts, and he lived among people suffering from extreme poverty. From those experiences, he came to realize the error of his ways and regret his violent past. He returned to Japan, passed his high school equivalency test, and entered a prestigious university. After graduating, he became a middle school English teacher. It's said that he chose to teach middle school because he wanted to help students avoid the kinds of mistakes he had made when he was that age. A few years ago he started spending his evenings in the video-game centers and bookstores where students get into trouble after school. He would seek them out one by one, talking to them about self-respect and offering them a chance to start over. He was so persistent he acquired the nickname Mr. Second Chance, and they even made a TV documentary about him. He published books and expanded the scope of his work, trying to reach more students—what's that? You heard all that on TV last week? Well, my apologies to those of you who already know the story.... What? You're right, I left out an important point. At the end of last year, when Sakuranomi was barely thirty-three years old, his doctor told him he had only a few months to live. But instead of feeling sorry for himself, he decided to devote his remaining time to his students. So now they've given him a new nickname: the Saint. You seem to know all about it, Mr. Abe. What's that? Do I *admire* Sakuranomi? Do I want to be like him? Those are tricky questions. I suppose you could say I want to learn from his life—but only the latter half.

But I can see what an impression he's made on some of you, and it makes me realize that I may have been an inadequate teacher in certain ways, especially compared to someone with his total dedication. As I said before, when I first became a teacher I wanted to do the best job I could. If one of my students had a problem, I would ignore my lesson plan and try to get the class to solve it together. If a student ran out of the room, even right in the middle of class, I would go after him. But at some point I started to realize that no one is perfect—me least of all. And when you tell a young person something with all the authority of a teacher, you actually risk amplifying the trouble. I began to feel that there was nothing more self-indulgent and foolish than forcing my opinions on my students. In the end, I worried I was simply condescending to the very people I should have been respecting and trying to help. So after my leave of absence, when I started work here at S Middle School, I laid down a couple of new ground rules for myself: First, I decided I would always address my students politely and use Mr. and Miss before their names, and second, I would treat them as equals. These seem like small things, but you'd be surprised how many students noticed right away.

Noticed what, you ask? I suppose they noticed how it made them feel to be treated with respect. You hear so much about abusive families that you might think that all children are being persecuted at home. But the truth is that most children these days are coddled and spoiled. Their parents bow and scrape and beg them to study, to eat their supper, whatever. Which may be why children show so little respect in return, why they talk to adults in the same tone of voice they use with their friends. And a lot of teachers even play up to this—consider it a badge of honor to be given a nickname or to be addressed informally by their students in class.

That's what they see on TV, after all, with all those shows about popular teachers who are "buddies" to their students. I'm sure you know how the plot goes—a popular teacher has trouble with one particular class, but out of the conflict a deep trust develops between them. And when the end credits roll, the rest of the school and the teacher's other classes have vanished and it's as though the teacher's there for that one group of troublemakers alone. Even in class, the TV teacher talks about his personal life and delves into the problem student's most intimate feelings. Do the rest of you want to hear all this? Oh yes, of course we do. Then some serious student gathers the courage to ask about the meaning of life...and then the drivel continues. In the last scene, the serious student usually ends up apologizing to the troublemaker for having been insensitive...which might be fine for TV, but how about in real life? Have any of you ever had a personal issue that seemed so pressing that you wanted to interrupt class to talk about it? There's too great an emphasis placed on the sheep gone astray. Personally, I have more respect for the serious student, the one who never got into trouble in the first place. But those kids never get the starring roles, either on TV or in real life. It's enough to make the well-behaved student doubt the value of his efforts.

People often talk about the sense of trust that develops between a teacher and her students. When my students started getting cell phones, I began to receive text messages saying things like: "I want to die" or "I have no reason to live"—cries for help. They often came in the middle of the night—two or three o'clock in the morning—and I have to admit I was tempted to ignore them. But of course I never could. That would have been betraying our "sense of trust."

Of course, teachers also started getting much more malicious messages. A young male teacher got a text asking for his help. The sender said her friend was in trouble and asked him to come to the entrance of a seedy hotel in the center of town. Now, you might think he should have been a little more cautious, but he was young and earnest and he hurried off to help—only to be photographed with the girl in the compromising location. Her parents showed up at the school the next day, the police got involved, and it turned into a major incident. His fellow teachers knew, of course, that the poor fellow had simply been tricked. We knew because he had told us that he was transgender—he had been born with the body of a man but he was actually a woman. Even under these circumstances, however, we saw no reason to reveal the truth. The young man himself, however, was determined to defend his honor as a teacher, and he ended up telling his students and their parents. But this whole tragedy—and the disastrous outcome for the teacher—had started from almost nothing. From a student's hurt feelings at having been told to stop talking during class.

What? Was the student ever punished? Of course not. On the contrary, the teacher and the school were blamed—how could they expose impressionable young people to sexual deviants...or gays...or even single mothers like myself? The parents ignored what their own daughter had done and blamed the school, and in the end they won—though I'm not sure it's ever appropriate to talk about winners and losers in a situation like this. The teacher? He was transferred last year and teaches at another school now, as a woman.

I know it's an extreme example, but these kinds of accusations get made all the time, and for male teachers they're very difficult to disprove. Since that incident, we've made it a policy to have a female teacher go in place of a male teacher when he has to meet with a female student, and vice versa. That's also why we have two male and two female teachers for each grade. If one of you boys were to ask me to meet you somewhere, I would immediately get in touch with Tokura-sensei from the A Class and ask him to go in my place; and if something happened involving a girl from the A Class, Tokura-sensei would contact me. You hadn't realized? There was never an announcement made, but we thought you'd figure it out for yourselves.

So now you boys are probably wondering whether it's even worth contacting me when you're really in trouble if

Tokura-sensei is going to show up anyway? What's that, Mr. Hasegawa? Yes, I remember when you had that problem in gym class. You told me it was serious, but in the bigger scheme of things it was quite minor. In fact, I doubt it's more than a few times a year when one of you really needs me. I'm sure when you text me saying you want to die, you truly believe on some level that "life has no meaning," as you all seem to like to say. And I'm sure that from your own self-absorbed point of view, you feel as though you're all alone in the great wide world. That your troubles are completely overwhelming. But I have to say that I'm less interested in catering to your adolescent whims and more concerned that you grow up someday to be people who are capable of considering the feelings of others—for example, the feelings of the person who receives such a thoughtless message in the middle of the night. To be honest, I doubt that anyone who was truly despondent, who was actually considering doing something drastic, would send an email to announce the fact to her teacher.

You may have guessed by now that I was never the sort of teacher who thought about her students twenty-four hours a day. There was always someone more important to me—my daughter, Manami. As you know, I was a single mother. Shortly before Manami's father and I were planning to be married, I learned that I was pregnant. We were a little disappointed that it had turned into a "shotgun wedding," as they say, but the truth is we were delighted at the prospect of having a baby. I began getting prenatal care, and we decided it would make sense for my fiancé to have a physical as well. Quite unexpectedly, the tests revealed that he was suffering from a terrible disease, and all talk of the wedding stopped at that point. Because of the illness? Of course, that was the reason. Was it hard for him to accept? I'm sure it was, Miss Isaka. And of course some couples go ahead and get married even though one of them is ill. They choose to face the problem together. But what would you do in this situation? What would you do if you found out your boyfriend or girlfriend was infected with HIV? ... HIV—the human immunodeficiency virus—better known as AIDS. But most of you already know all about this from the novel you read for your summer project. So many of your book reports said that you had cried at the ending that I decided to read it for myself. For the few of you who chose another book, it's about a girl who contracts HIV while working as a prostitute and eventually develops AIDS and dies.

What's that? You don't think the story is that simple? You found the woman—the heroine—more sympathetic than I made her sound? I can understand that, but if you sympathized with the girl in the book, why did so many of you push your chairs back just now when I told you what happened with my fiancé? If you're so sympathetic to people with AIDS, why did you move away when you found out that the teacher standing in front of you had sex with someone infected with HIV?

You look particularly uncomfortable, Miss Hamazaki, sitting here in the front row, but there's no need to hold your breath. HIV is not spread through the air. The fact is you can't catch AIDS from most kinds of physical contact—not from shaking hands or coughing or sneezing, not from the bath or the swimming pool, not from sharing dishes or from mosquito bites or from your pets. In general, not even from kissing. You can't get AIDS from living in close contact with an infected person, and no one has *ever* caught it simply by being in the same class with someone who was infected—though I know the book didn't mention any of that. And I apologize for keeping you in suspense—but I'm not infected, either. Don't look so shocked. It's true that sexual intercourse is one way of spreading HIV, but not every act of intercourse results in infection.

I was tested during my pregnancy and the results were negative, but because that seemed so hard to believe, I was retested several times. It was only later, when I learned the real infection rate from intercourse, that I understood why I had escaped, but I won't tell you that figure since I know how easily influenced you are by statistics. If you want to know, you're free to look it up yourselves.

My fiancé contracted HIV overseas, during a wild period in his life when he hadn't cared much what happened to him. I'm afraid I found it difficult to accept this part of his past. It had been a terrible shock to learn that the man I was planning to marry was infected with HIV, and despite the tests I continued to worry that I was infected, too. Even after I was sure that I was safe, I lay awake at night worrying about the baby in my belly. While I never stopped respecting my lover, I have to say that at times I truly hated him for what he'd done. And I suppose he could sense that. He apologized to me repeatedly and pleaded with me to go ahead and have the baby. But I have to say that the thought of ending the pregnancy never crossed my mind. Irrespective of politics, it felt like murder to me.

I should also tell you that my fiancé didn't dissolve into self-pity after learning he had AIDS. On the contrary, he seemed to feel that he was simply suffering the consequences of his actions, and he was always careful to distinguish between his situation and that of hemophiliacs and others who had contracted the virus through no fault of their own. Still, I can't imagine the despair he must have been feeling.

Eventually I realized I'd been wrong—partly because I so much wanted my baby to have a father—and I told him that we should go through with the wedding, that as long as we both understood the situation, we would find a way to face the problem. But he refused quite stubbornly. He was strong-willed, and he was absolutely determined to put the child's happiness above all else. Prejudice against people with HIV is terrible in Japan—if you want proof, just remember how you all held your breath a moment ago when you thought I was infected. Even if the child turned out to be HIV-negative, how would she be treated when it was learned that the father had AIDS? If she made friends, would their parents forbid them to play with her? When she was old enough to go to school, would the other children—or even the teachers—mistreat her and try to force her out of the cafeteria or gym class or anywhere they thought a problem might occur? Of course, a child with no father can also experience prejudice, but the challenges are much less serious and she has a much better chance of finally winning acceptance. At any rate, we decided to call off the wedding. I was left to raise our daughter alone.

After she was born, Manami was tested and turned out to be HIV-negative as well. You can't imagine how relieved I was. I made up my mind to give her the best care a mother could, to protect her at all costs, and I poured every ounce of my love into her. If you were to ask me which was more important, my students or my daughter, I would have answered without a moment's hesitation that my daughter was far more important. Which was, of course, only natural.

Manami asked me about her father only once. I told her that he was working very hard, so hard he couldn't come see her. And this was, in fact, quite true. Having given up the right to call himself Manami's father, he had thrown himself into his work as though the rest of his life depended on it. But his sacrifice was meaningless in the end.

Manami is no longer with us.

When Manami turned one, I put her into day care and returned to teaching. In the city, day care centers will keep a child until late into the evening, but out here in the countryside, even extended care ends at six o'clock. So I consulted a placement service for seniors looking for part-time work and found Mrs. Takenaka. She lives just behind the school swimming pool. Yes, that's right, the house with the big black dog named Muku. I'm sure some of you have fed Muku your leftovers from lunch through the fence.

At four o'clock when the day care center closed, Mrs.

Takenaka would go to get Manami and keep her for me until I finished work. The two of them grew very attached to one another. Manami loved Mrs. Takenaka and called her Grannie, and she loved Muku, too, and was very proud of the fact that she was often given the job of feeding him. This arrangement continued for three years, but at the beginning of this year, Mrs. Takenaka fell ill and went into the hospital.

Because we had been so close, I felt uncomfortable looking for a replacement simply because she was laid up for a few weeks, so I decided that I would go get Manami from the day care center myself until Mrs. Takenaka got well. In general this worked well enough, since they were willing to keep Manami until six o'clock and I was usually able to wrap things up at school by then. But on Wednesdays, our faculty meetings often went later, so on those days I would get Manami at four o'clock and have her wait for me in the nurse's office. Miss Naitō and Miss Matsukawa, you often played with her while she was there, didn't you? I'm truly grateful to you for that. She loved those afternoons. She told me that you girls said she looked like her favorite cartoon character, Snuggly Bunny. She couldn't have been more delighted.

Please don't cry, girls. Those are happy memories.

Manami loved rabbits, and she loved anything that was soft and fluffy. So of course she was crazy about Snuggly Bunny—though in that she was no different from most of the girls in Japan, even those in high school. Just about everything she owned—her backpack, her hankies, her shoes, even her socks, had his little face printed on it. She would climb up on my lap every morning with her little Snuggly Bunny hair bands and ask me to make her look like Bunny, and on weekends when we went shopping, she would always spot some new sort of Snuggly Bunny product that made her eyes sparkle.

About a week before Manami died, we had gone out to the shopping center. There was a Valentine's display with all kinds of chocolate, including a whole selection with especially cute packaging, probably for girls to give to one another instead of to boys. Manami was drawn to the display and immediately spotted a Snuggly Bunny–shaped bar of white chocolate that came in a Snuggly Bunny–shaped fuzzy pouch. Of course, she wanted me to buy it for her, but we had a rule that she could only buy one item when we went shopping, and I'd already bought her a Snuggly Bunny sweatshirt that day—the pink one she was wearing the day she died. I told her she could get the chocolate bunny the next time we came shopping and began to lead her away from the candy.

Normally she would have followed me quietly enough. But for some reason that day was different. She sat down on the floor in the middle of the store and began to cry, telling me that she didn't want the sweatshirt and that I had to buy her the chocolate. But a rule is a rule, and I wasn't about to let her get away with that kind of behavior. I told myself I would buy it for her another time, when I was alone, and give it to her on Valentine's Day. I reminded her about our rule and told her that she needed to behave herself. As a mother, I'd had to learn that there was a clear difference between loving your child and spoiling her. But just then Mr. Shitamura happened to appear from somewhere. You had apparently been watching the whole thing, since you came up and offered your opinion without being asked. You seemed to think I was being unreasonable to deny Manami something that cost only ¥700. Fortunately, Manami was embarrassed to have you see her sitting on the floor having a tantrum, and she immediately calmed down and stood up. "Okay," she said, puffing out those little cheeks, "but next time I'm getting it for sure." Then she gave you a smile and a little wave and we left.

Of course, with Manami gone before Valentine's ever came, I regret not buying her that chocolate every day.

The faculty meeting ended just before six o'clock that day. The school nurses attended the meeting, so their office was empty. But several of you girls were kind enough to look after Manami until the school closed at six, so she never complained about being bored or lonely, and she was always waiting patiently for me when I got out of the meeting. That day, however, she wasn't in the office. I checked the restroom, but she wasn't there, either. It was just as after-school activities were winding up, and it occurred to me she might have gone to find some of you girls in your club rooms, so I wandered around the school looking for her, not particularly concerned at that point. I ran into Miss Naitō and Miss Matsukawa, and you told me that you'd gone to play with Manami in the nurse's office around five o'clock but that she hadn't been there. You'd thought she hadn't come to school that day. Then you helped me look for her.

It was dark by then, but there were still a number of people in the school, and they all joined in the search that evening. Mr. Hoshino, you were the one who found her—after you'd finished with baseball practice. You said you hadn't seen her that day but that you remembered seeing her once coming from the direction of the pool, and you went there with me to look for her. The gate was chained for the winter, so we climbed the fence, but the chain was loose enough to let someone as small as Manami slip through. The pool was full, even though swimming classes were over for the year. The water was cloudy and dark—it had been kept in case it was needed to fight a fire.

We found Manami floating on the surface. We pulled her out as quickly as we could, but her body was icy and her heart had stopped. Still, I continued to call her name and perform CPR. Despite the shock of seeing Manami's body, Mr. Hoshino went right away to call the other teachers. Manami was transported to the hospital, where she was pronounced dead. The cause of death was determined to be drowning. Since there were no injuries or any sign that she'd been attacked, the police concluded that she had fallen in accidentally.

It was already dark when we found Manami and I was terribly upset, so there's no reason I should have noticed this, but I did remember seeing Muku's nose poking through the fence that separated Mrs. Takenaka's yard from the pool. The police investigation turned up bread crumbs in that area, from the same sort of bread they served at Manami's day care center. Several students testified that they had seen Manami in the vicinity of the pool, and it became clear that she had been in the habit of going there every week. The neighbors were taking care of Muku while Mrs. Takenaka was in the hospital, but Manami had no way of knowing that, and she may have thought that the dog would starve if she didn't bring him the bread. She must have been worried that I would scold her if I found out, so she always went alone and tried to avoid being noticed. According to the students who had seen these little excursions, she was never gone more than ten minutes or so.

Of course, I had no idea about any of this. When I would ask her what she did while she was waiting for me, she'd give me a mischievous look and tell me she'd been playing with some of you girls. I should have realized then that she was hiding something and questioned her more. If I had, she might never have gone to the pool.

Manami died because I was supposed to be looking out for her and I wasn't vigilant enough. I am truly sorry, too, for the shock it caused everyone here at the school. It's been more than a month now, and I still reach out on the futon every morning, expecting to find Manami curled up next to me. When we went to sleep at night, she would always push up against me, making sure that we were touching somewhere; and if I pulled away to tease her, she would reach out toward me again. When I relented and took her hand, she would relax and drop off to sleep. I find myself crying now each morning when I reach out and realize that I will never again feel her downy cheeks or her soft hair.

When I told the principal I would be resigning, he asked

whether it was because of what happened to Manami—
which is just what you were wondering earlier, Miss Kitahara. And it's true that I've decided to resign because of
Manami's death. But it's also true that under other circumstances I would probably have continued to teach in order to
atone for what I'd done and to take my mind off my misery.
So why am I resigning?

Because Manami's death wasn't an accident. She was murdered by some of the students in this very class.

I wonder how much you know about the age limits society
imposes on certain things, and how you feel about them. For
example, how old do you have to be to buy alcohol and to-
bacco? Mr. Nishio? That's right, twenty years old. I'm glad
you're aware of these rules. People are legally considered
adults when they reach the age of twenty, and every year the
TV news covers the crop of newly minted citizens as they
drink too much and make fools of themselves at New Year's,
when they celebrate their majority.

Now, it may seem odd that these young people are all
overindulging right on cue, right at this one moment in their
lives, and of course the fact that the TV cameras show up to
film them has something to do with it. But it's also true that
this whole spectacle would probably never have developed if
we didn't have the rule that people aren't allowed to drink
until they turn twenty. The fact that society permits the con-
sumption of alcohol at twenty doesn't mean it actively recom-
mends that its members drink—or get drunk. Nevertheless,
the legal age limit for drinking no doubt plays an important

role in promoting the notion that you're somehow missing out on something if you *don't* drink once you're old enough to do so—even if you don't particularly feel like drinking in the first place. Still, I suppose the age limit does serve some purpose—without it, some of you might actually be showing up drunk for class here at the middle school. And I suppose some of you couldn't care less about the law anyway and have already started drinking, perhaps at the urging of an uncle or an older friend. So I suppose it's too idealistic to think that people can be left to develop their own sense of ethics.

But maybe I'm being too vague. Maybe you can't see what it is that I'm trying to tell you.

Or rather, you're so busy wondering who the murderer could be that you can't think about anything else. You may feel a little afraid to be here in the same room with someone who was capable of this kind of crime, but I suspect it's really your curiosity that's got the better of you now. I can also tell from the looks on your faces that some of you may have guessed who the murderers are and some of you actually know. I have to admit, though, that what shocks me is to see the murderers sitting there so calmly while I'm up here saying all this to you.

But perhaps "shocks" isn't quite the right word. I suppose I'm not really shocked at all. Because I also know that one of the two murderers actually wanted his name to become known. While the other—the one who went pale a few minutes ago when I said I knew what they'd done—looks as though he's about to faint. But don't worry. I'm not going to reveal your names now, in front of the class.

You all know something about the Juvenile Law, don't you?

The law was written with the idea that young people are still immature and in the process of becoming adults, so when necessary, the state, in place of parents, needs to find the best way to rehabilitate those who commit crimes. When I was young, this meant that a child under sixteen who committed a crime—even if it was murder—was handed over to Family Court and usually didn't even end up in a juvenile facility. But that view of children as pure and innocent seems outdated now. The Juvenile Law got turned on its head in the 1990s when fourteen- and fifteen-year-olds began to commit the most horrible crimes on a regular basis. You were just a few years old, but I'm sure many of you have heard of the incident in Kobe where a young man, still a child himself, killed several other children, beheading one of them. I'm sure the rest of you would know what I'm talking about if I mentioned the name that the killer used in the threatening notes he wrote. That case and others like it started a debate about the need to revise the Juvenile Law, and in April of 2001 a new version was passed that included lowering the age of criminal responsibility from sixteen to fourteen.

But most of you are thirteen. What, then, does age mean, exactly?

I suspect you remember a more recent incident, the story of the poisoning of that whole family last year. The young girl who did it was just your age, thirteen, and in her first year of middle school. During summer vacation she started mixing some sort of poison into the family dinner and then writing in her blog about any changes she noticed in her victims. But it seems that the effects of the poison were disappointing, so she ended up adding potassium cyanide to the curry one evening and killing her parents, her grandmother, and her little brother, who was just in fourth grade. You may remember the last line on her blog: "Cyanide did the trick!" The newspapers and TV were full of this story for weeks. That's right, Miss Sonezaki, it was called the Lunacy Incident—I'm sure you recognize that name. In Roman mythology, Luna referred to the moon or the moon goddess. The word *lunacy* itself came to mean "insanity" or "psychosis" or even "foolish behavior." The TV and newspapers picked up on the word because she had used it in her blog, and there was speculation that she must have had a split personality—how else would a quiet, serious young girl turn into the insane moon goddess?

The whole thing became a media circus. And I suspect some of you know what became of her, what sort of punishment she received. Despite the publicity and the fancy name given to the case, because she was a minor she was never identified and no pictures ever appeared in the press. All we had were exaggerated reports of her crime and vague conjectures about her dark mental state, and the whole thing faded away, with the truth completely unknown.

But does that kind of reporting, that sort of public information, seem adequate? All it succeeded in doing was planting knowledge of the existence of this sort of utterly inhuman criminal in the minds of some of our young people—and encouraging that pathetic minority of their peers who already admire or even worship that sort of senseless criminal. If you ask me, if we're going to suppress the names and photographs of underage criminals, we should also prevent publication of the flashy aliases they assume to advertise their crimes. She called herself "Lunacy" on her blog, but since she could only be identified as "Ms. A" in the press, perhaps they should come up with some sort of humiliating alias for her blog name as well. They could blur over "Lunacy" or replace it with "Loser" or "Idiot." In the same way, for that beheading case in Kobe, we should have been laughing at that pathetic boy's pretentious use of fancy characters and ridiculous designs for the signature in his notes.

I wonder what sort of image comes to mind when people try to imagine what the Lunacy girl looks like. Think about it for a moment. Would a beautiful young woman call herself a lunatic? If the law says you can't print a picture of an underage murderer, why let people imagine someone pretty? Print a fake picture instead of a hideous, grinning, evil-minded lunatic. Why not show exactly what this sort of human being is like? If we choose instead to coddle them and make a fuss over them, aren't we just fueling their narcissism? And won't there be even more foolish kids out there to idolize them? Above all, when a child commits this sort of crime, isn't it the responsibility of the adult world to handle it as discreetly as possible and to make the criminal understand its seriousness in no uncertain terms? That Lunacy girl will spend a few years in a juvenile facility somewhere, perhaps write an apology of some sort, and then be released back into society knowing she literally got away with murder.

You may not know this, but the harshest criticism during that incident wasn't for the girl herself but for the science teacher at her middle school. I'll call him T to protect his privacy, but it was well known that T was an unusually conscientious teacher whose primary concern was his students' academic achievement, and that he had complained more than once that the science curriculum was becoming obsessed with safety, to the point where only innocuous, harmless experiments were allowed in the classroom.

Did I know him? Actually, I had a chance to talk with him at the National Middle School Science Fair just a few days before the incident became known. The girl told T that she had left her notebook in the classroom and asked whether she could go pick it up. He was in the middle of a parent-teacher conference, and since the girl was a good student and well behaved, he'd handed her his whole key ring without a second thought. It later came out that she'd bought most of the chemicals in her poison cocktail at the local pharmacy or online, but she'd gotten the potassium cyanide from school—and T was universally condemned for being too lax in managing such a dangerous substance.

It didn't stop there. There were even ugly—false—rumors that he had tempted the girl, led her on, and he was soon forced out of his job. He's still suffering the effects even though the media attention has died down. His wife, who couldn't deal with the endless slander, is in a hospital somewhere for nervous exhaustion, and his little boy has adopted his mother's surname and gone to live with an aunt in another prefecture. Not long after, a notice went out to all the science teachers from the school board ordering us to make inventories of all controlled or potentially hazardous substances.

Strictly speaking, you don't need potassium cyanide in a middle school science lab, and, though T might have had his reasons for keeping it around, I can understand questioning his judgment for surrendering the keys so easily. Still, while we don't have potassium cyanide here at our school, we've got lots of other things that could be used to kill someone. We do keep the key to the chemical locker in a cupboard that students don't have access to, but if someone were willing to shatter the glass on the door, who could say what might happen? Even if you eliminated every dangerous chemical, you'd still have the knives in the cafeteria kitchen, and the jump ropes out in the field house. Even those could be used to strangle someone. Nor do we teachers have the right to confiscate your property, even if we're quite sure you have a knife. You may be bringing it with the express purpose of hurting a classmate, but if you simply say you were carrying it to protect yourself from a bully on the way to school, we have no recourse. And if we report our concerns up the line, we're told we should just "be more vigilant." Only when your knife causes an accident or is used to hurt someone do we finally have the right to take it away from you—but it's too late by then, and inevitably someone will criticize us for not preventing the tragedy if we knew about the knife. Who is really to blame here? Is it really the fault of negligent teachers?

Was Manami's death really my fault? What was I supposed to do?

*　　*　　*

Manami's funeral was private and as quiet as possible. I know a number of you wanted to attend, and I'm sorry that we could not invite you. Part of me wanted to have a large number of people present to say good-bye to her, but I felt even more strongly that it was important to allow her father to be there. They had only met once before, at the end of last year. I hadn't even realized it had happened until I was watching television with Manami one evening and she suddenly pointed at the screen.

"I met that man yesterday," she said. I thought my heart was going to stop. When I asked her what she meant, she said that the man had been outside the fence at her preschool, apparently watching her as she played on the swings. He had gotten her attention and waved for her to come over to the fence, so she went. She'd been surprised that he knew her name, and he asked her whether she was happy. When she said she was, he had smiled. "I'm glad," he told her and then he had walked away.

I'm quite certain that the man was Manami's father. The security at the preschool has been tightened recently, and even residents of the neighborhood are checked out if they're seen lingering too long outside the fences. Still, Manami's father would hardly have aroused suspicion. And even if someone had stopped him, he could have made up some sort of excuse—and as soon as he was recognized, he would have been invited right in as a famous teacher.

After hearing Manami's story, I started wondering how

her father was getting along, and for the first time since we'd parted—for the first time in five years—I called him. That was when I learned that he had finally begun to suffer from the symptoms of AIDS. The character in the book you read fell ill almost immediately, but in reality the virus often has an incubation period of between five and ten years. In his case, it had taken almost fourteen years, which is apparently remarkably long. At any rate, I wasn't quite sure what to say when he told me, but before I could answer he promised in a lifeless voice that he would never try to see Manami again. There was no trace in his tone of the energetic man you see on TV. I asked if he would like to go away somewhere with Manami and me over winter break. It wasn't an offer made out of pity for a dying man—I simply wanted to spend time as a real family. But he declined in the same lifeless tone.

The first time he ever hugged Manami was after she was already dead. He came to watch with me the evening after she died, and he held her and wept and blamed his past sins for what had happened. They say you can only cry until your tears dry up, but that never seemed to happen to us. We found ourselves hoping in vain for an end to the tears, and bitterly regretting that we had never made time for the three of us to be together.

It seems that I've been telling you a great deal about my regrets this afternoon.

After the funeral, a great many people came to our house to pay their final respects. Her preschool teachers and class-mates, and so many others. We asked them not to bring the traditional condolence money, but they brought Snuggly

Bunny dolls and candy and left those instead in front of Manami's photograph. I'm sure she sleeps easier surrounded by her favorite bunny — or so I tell myself.

Mrs. Takenaka came to visit me just last week, as soon as she got out of the hospital, exactly a month after Manami died. She knelt in front of our household altar and wept and apologized to Manami's spirit. She had read in the local papers that Manami had crept into the pool area to feed a dog, and she was devastated by a sense that she was somehow responsible for Manami's death. Since the incident had occurred on school property and because I was so exhausted, I had let the principal check the newspaper story before it was published rather than doing it myself, but after seeing Mrs. Takenaka I regretted that. There they are again — more regrets.

Mrs. Takenaka had gathered up all the things Manami had left at her house and brought them to me in a paper bag. A change of clothes and underwear, her chopsticks and spoon, stuffed animals and a few small toys. But among these familiar objects, which were now painful mementos, was one that was not so familiar: a pouch in the shape of Snuggly Bunny's head made out of soft velour. It was the one Manami had begged for at the store, the one I had refused to buy her — but what was it doing in Mrs. Takenaka's bag? Manami had always told me when Mrs. Takenaka or anyone else had given her something, even if it was no more than a piece of candy. The pouch, Mrs. Takenaka said, had turned up in Muku's doghouse, which might explain why it was frayed in places. But she had worried that Manami would miss it, so she had brought it to put on the altar despite its condition.

I thanked her for all the kindness she had shown Manami and for coming to see me before she had fully recovered, and then I drove her home. Muku was playing with a baseball in the overgrown yard. Mrs. Takenaka said that the ball had come from the school, but it struck me as unlikely that even the best batter on the team could have hit a home run that would have cleared the nets and the pool and landed in her yard. She explained that she had sometimes seen students who were cleaning the pool area after school playing catch on the pool deck, and that the ball was probably theirs. The punishment for minor infractions at school was cleanup duty at the pool or the sports sheds, and I had forgotten that some of you in this very class had received this punishment during the past few months.

Was Manami alone at the pool that day? I suddenly began to have my doubts. Back home, I took a closer look at the Snuggly Bunny pouch. Had it really belonged to Manami? If so, who had bought it for her? As I held it in my hand, I realized it was oddly heavy. Unzipping it, I discovered what seemed to be a metal coil visible under the thin cloth of the lining. Fighting back a horrible suspicion, I went to school the next day and brought in two students for separate interviews....

From the noise in the hall it sounds as though the other classes have let out. If any of you have club activities or have to go to cram school, or if you simply want to leave, please do so. I know this has been unpleasant and that I've gone on a long while now. What I have to say from here on out is even more unpleasant, so if you don't want to hear, please leave. No one? Then I'll take that to mean that you are all staying of your own free will.

I'll call the two killers A and B from here on.

There was nothing in particular that drew my attention to A in the first months he was here at school. Apparently he had managed to impress some of the other boys in this class, but I didn't know that, and I didn't notice him until after the midterm exams during the first quarter. He scored a perfect one hundred percent, and, since he was the only one in the entire grade to do so, his scores became known not just to those of you in his homeroom but to other classes as well. I know that most of you were proud of him, but I found out that there was some grumbling in those other classes. A comment made by another child—let's call him C—was reported back to me. C had apparently gone to elementary school with A, and he said that A had an unfair advantage since he was "doing 'live' experiments." I was disturbed to hear this, so I had C come talk with me in the science room. Before he agreed to tell me what he knew, he insisted I tell no one else. Then he described A's activities during the last year of elementary school, how he had gathered stray cats and dogs from the neighborhood and, using a device he invented and dubbed the Execution Machine, he had tortured and finally killed the animals. At first C had spoken quietly, looking down at the desk, but as he talked he got more and more excited. "He took pictures of the dead animals and *posted them on his website!*" he concluded, as if describing his own exploits, and I remember shuddering to see how much he admired what A had done.

I had him tell me A's website address before he left, and then I went straight to the computer in the teachers' office to have a look. There was nothing there but a message in a forbidding font saying that "A new machine is currently under development." There had been nothing about any of this in the files that were sent over from the elementary school when A started here, but I took the precaution of phoning his sixth grade homeroom teacher. "No, I never heard anything like that. He was a serious student and his grades were excellent," he said, apparently unconcerned by my call. In the weeks that followed, I kept an eye on A, but he was, as I'd been told, a serious boy who seemed to have a good attitude toward school and life in general—all in all, a model student—and before long I went back to paying very little attention to him. You can call me naïve, but I suppose I had my hands full elsewhere.

One day toward the middle of last June I was alone in the science lab preparing an experiment for the ninth grade class when A came to see me. He examined the lab equipment with apparent interest, and then he asked me what I had studied in college. When I told him I had majored in chemistry, he asked how much I knew about electrical devices. I had done courses in physics as well, but remembering that A's father owned an electronics shop, I told him that I doubted I knew as much as he did.

At this, he suddenly held out a small, black imitation-leather coin purse with a zipper. It looked perfectly innocent, the type of thing you could buy anywhere. I wondered what he wanted me to do with it, but when I looked up he was leering at me. "Open it," he said. "There's a surprise inside." I knew it was a trick of some sort and took it from him very carefully. It seemed a bit heavy for its size and I was sure there must, in fact, be something inside. Telling myself I wasn't going to be shocked by a frog or a spider, I gripped the tab on the zipper, but as I did a strong shock went through my fingers. For a moment I thought it was static electricity, but I quickly realized that was unlikely on a rainy day in June. As I stood looking at the purse and my fingers, A spoke up.

"Pretty amazing, isn't it? It took me more than three months to make." He sounded proud of himself. "Still, the shock wasn't as strong as I thought it would be."

I couldn't believe what I was hearing.

"You mean you were using me as your guinea pig?"

"What's the big deal?" he said, still grinning and as calm as ever. "Don't people take drugs or get shocked all the time for chemistry and biology experiments? As long as you control the amount."

I remembered what C had told me, and that A's website said his new machine was under development.

"Why are you making a dangerous thing like this?" I asked him. "What are you planning to do with it? Kill small animals?" My fingers were still tingling from the shock.

A made an exaggerated show of being surprised, like some comedian miming astonishment. "Why do you have to be so touchy?" he said. "I can't believe you don't see how great this is. Just forget it. I'll show it to someone else, someone who'll appreciate it." He snatched the purse out of my hand and left.

At the faculty meeting that week I reported that A had made a purse with an electrified zipper and explained how dangerous it could be, and I relayed what C had told me about A's activities in elementary school. But they seemed to think I was talking about something equivalent to a static shock, and the principal just said to give him a stern warning and be vigilant. I also called A's house to talk with his parents, not to accuse A but to let them know that his experiments could be dangerous and ask them to keep an eye on his activities. His mother didn't take kindly to the call.

"I'm impressed you have so much free time to be calling me about this," she said, her voice dripping with irony. "Especially since you've got your own child to look after."

I started checking A's website daily. I was sure that when he'd said he'd show it to "someone else" what he'd really meant was that he'd post it there. But the site continued to say the device was under development.

The next week A showed up again with the purse, a thick file, and a paper, which he wanted me to sign. It turned out to be an entry form for the National Middle School Science Fair—the one advertised in the poster at the back of the room. The deadline was the end of June. Since the projects were due before summer vacation, I had simply mentioned the competition briefly in class. It had never occurred to me that A would want to enter his purse.

In the blank for the title, he had written, "Theft-Prevention *Shocking* Coin Purse." Under "Objectives": "To protect my precious allowance from thieves." The blanks were all filled in except for the name and signature of the project advisor. From the project design section of the entry materials in the file, I could see that he had added a safety catch to the purse that would allow the owner to handle it, while anyone trying to open the zipper would be shocked. There was also a detailed explanation of the design and manufacturing process, with elaborate illustrations.

At the end, he had written about the remaining problems, primarily the fact that the purse would deliver only a single shock. He proposed to continue working on the design as he developed "college-level, specialized knowledge," and he concluded with what I took to be an intentionally childish flourish: "I'll keep trying to improve my invention until even my grandmother can use it with peace of mind!" The application was written out by hand, though I knew A had a computer at home, and I could see that it had been carefully calculated to suggest the earnest efforts of a middle school boy.

"I know you didn't really help me with it," A said, after I'd had a quick look at the application. "But I have to have someone sign it, and you're my homeroom teacher and you teach science. Please?" When I hesitated, looking down at the entry form, he went on. "I made it for all the right reasons. I just want to protect kids' stuff. But you say it's dangerous. Why don't we let the experts decide who's right?" It sounded like a challenge, almost a declaration of war. In the end, he won and I lost. The Theft-Prevention *Shocking* Coin Purse received the Governor's Award at the prefectural level and went on to the national competition. There it was lavishly praised and took honorable mention in the middle school division, the equivalent of third place in the whole country.

I called A to the science lab to find out the truth about Manami's death. At the time, I thought I could actually accomplish something by doing this. I suppose I was trying to deal with my own feelings of guilt.

He came around noon, after a half day of school, with an innocent grin on his face. I held out the Snuggly Bunny pouch.

"Open it. There's a surprise inside," I told him, repeating his invitation to me, but of course he refused to touch it. A shame, really. I had made my own improvements, increasing the power to the level of a stun gun. It wasn't difficult to do. With a little research, anybody could make something like this—the real question is why anyone would want to.

When he realized why I had called him, he began telling the whole tale in a tone that was almost triumphant, as though he had been waiting for this day all along. The coin purse that he'd taken to the science fair was, as I'd suspected, the prototype of his Execution Machine.

When he'd finished the first model, he had tried it out on his video game friends. They'd been impressed but not enough to satisfy A. He wasn't showing them a jack-in-the-box. They were incapable of understanding what he'd accomplished, so he decided to show it to someone who could appreciate it. That's when he brought it to me. My reaction did satisfy him, but that was a misunderstanding on his part.

It wasn't the purse that had frightened me but A himself, his whole way of looking at the world. But he was convinced the purse had scared me, and intentionally provoked me before he left, thinking I would spread the word about his dangerous invention to the other teachers and his classmates. He was mistaken again. I did report the incident, as I've said, but no one else seemed the least bit interested. It occurred to A, of course, that he could present his invention on his website, but he was afraid no one would understand it, so he decided to take it to people who could properly appreciate it.

That's how it came to be entered in the Science Fair. The judges were mostly professors with impressive titles from technical universities, and A fully expected these experts to be appalled by his lethal entry and to label it—and him— a menace. In this way he would have attracted the attention he so desperately wanted. But he hadn't wanted his project to be rejected on these grounds in the local, preliminary rounds, so he had crafted the accompanying materials to suggest that a childish—that is, age-appropriate—sense of justice motivated the booby-trapped purse. But he had apparently done his job too well, and both he and his invention were seen as perfectly wholesome right through to the national finals.

One of the judges at the national level, a well-known professor who has appeared on TV quiz shows, came up to A as he was standing by his exhibit in the hall and told him how impressed he was. "I couldn't have put together something like that myself," he apparently told him. The crime-stopping Shocking Purse had attracted attention as something a bit different in a sea of robot helpers of one sort or another.

But A misunderstood again. He thought he was being praised for his technical skills, an understandable misapprehension for a child to have. He still wasn't being recognized for the dangerous villain he wanted to be, but he took some satisfaction in being interviewed by the local newspapers. When I saw his picture and read about his success, I was somewhat relieved myself. I felt that he had only wanted a little recognition and attention, and that now that he'd gotten it, he might develop in a more positive direction. I decided that I had been unnecessarily concerned and that everything had worked out in the end.

One day late last summer, the local newspaper printed a long article about A's project and the science fair. But that same day the Lunacy Incident broke and the front pages were filled with the story. In the days that followed, the TV and the weekly magazines talked about almost nothing else. A's achievement was acknowledged in front of the whole school at the opening ceremony for the second quarter, but the fact that he had been praised by the famous professor and that the newspaper had written about him was hardly mentioned. The Lunacy Incident was all anyone could talk about. What did A care that they had said good things about him? No one had even noticed. And what was so great about the Lunacy thing? Potassium cyanide? It wasn't as though she had discovered it—who couldn't use a deadly poison to kill people? A had invented his own murder weapon. Shouldn't that get a lot more attention? But the more the media made a fuss over Lunacy, the more jealous A became, and the more he threw himself into developing his Execution Machine.

* * *

From the time he first entered school, B was a friendly, sociable child. He was pleasant and mild-mannered, exactly what one might expect of someone who had been carefully raised by his parents and two sisters, who were quite a bit older. When I had finished my interview with A, I called B to try to get him to meet me at the pool. Of course, from the meeting place itself he must have guessed my intention, and I was asked to come to his home instead. When I arrived, B said he wanted his mother to join us. She seemed surprised by my sudden appearance, from which I guessed that she had no idea what her son had done. I agreed that she could be present, and we began talking about B's experiences since he had first started middle school.

He had joined Tennis Club during his first quarter. He'd been interested in trying a sport, and tennis had struck him as "cool." But once the club had started, he discovered that it was already unfairly stratified. The kids who had played tennis in elementary school were almost immediately allowed to play on the courts, but those who had never played were relegated to a course of fitness training, and even after several weeks had gone by they still had never so much as touched a racket. B was in the latter group, but since it included more than half the kids, he hadn't been particularly upset. After a couple of months of practice, he was allowed to actually play, and he had started to like the way he looked carrying the racket case back and forth to school.

At the start of summer vacation, their coach, Mr. Tokura,

divided them into skills groups again and posted a practice regime for each. The groups included "Offensive skills," "Defensive skills," and the like, but B found himself once again grouped with the kids who were assigned to work on "Fitness skills." Worse still, while each of the other groups had six members, there were just two others in B's "Fitness" group: D, who stopped coming to practice almost immediately after the groups were posted, and E, a small, slender, pale boy who was known by the unflattering nickname "Kathy."

Day after day, B and Kathy ran laps around the school. Convinced that his own level of fitness was no worse than the kids in the other groups, B felt himself growing more and more frustrated. One day a girl from another club asked him why he was running all the time if he was in Tennis Club. Thoroughly humiliated, B went to Coach Tokura and asked to be moved to another group. The coach asked him whether he objected to the running itself or to being seen running with Kathy. It was, of course, the latter, but B couldn't tell the coach how he felt. "If you're always worrying about what other people think, you'll never get any tougher. Stick it out," the coach told him. "We'll be finishing group practices in another week." But the next day B's mother phoned the school to say he was quitting tennis, and soon after that he started attending an extremely competitive cram school all the way in town.

B's grades had never been better than simply average, but by the time we started the second quarter, he had moved quite a bit higher in the class rankings. His scores on the midterms were nearly fifteen points higher than those in the first quarter, and at the cram school as well, where the levels were divided by class standing, in two months he had jumped from the lowest group, Class 5, to Class 2, second from the top. F, whose grades were roughly the same as B's, started going to the same cram school in November. F started in Class 4.

Puberty is a time when a child's abilities—whether in academics or sports or the arts—may suddenly begin to develop at a rapid pace. Seeing these successes, the child may then develop a certain self-confidence in that field, which in turn encourages increased effort—and increased success. Of course, it also happens in many cases that the child overestimates his abilities—or, like an athlete who encounters a slump, the child often develops rapidly only to reach a plateau where the rate of increase tapers off drastically.

It's what happens next that really matters. Some children, convinced that they've reached the full extent of their abilities, stop trying and allow themselves to follow a downward curve to mediocrity. Others calmly continue to make the effort, regardless of results, and manage to maintain themselves at that level. But still others dig in and overcome the obstacle and eventually manage to move up to the next level. Those of us who serve as homeroom teachers for students preparing for the high school entrance exams are used to hearing parents tell us that their child could succeed if he would "just try." But more often than not, the child they're speaking of has reached this juncture and followed the downward curve. It's not so much that he hasn't tried; he's simply no longer even in the game.

B, too, arrived at this moment in his development.

By the time we were ready to go on winter break, his grades were no longer improving and had even begun to go down a bit. At the start of the third quarter, he was subjected to a pep talk by his cram school teacher in front of the whole class—something right out of a TV commercial. "You let yourself celebrate *waaay* too soon! A few As and you started to relax and it's right back to the old Bs and Cs!" B found the whole experience humiliating. What right did the man have to belittle him in front of everybody just because his grades had gone down a bit? But that wasn't the worst of it. When the teacher announced the new class assignments, B was still in the second level, while F had moved up to the top group. He was furious, and when the lessons were over that afternoon, he went straight to the game center to work off his anger and spend the money he had received for New Year's.

He was completely absorbed in a game when he suddenly realized he was surrounded by a group of high school students. They tried to take his wallet, he resisted, and when a patrol officer happened by and noticed the scuffle, he was taken into protective custody. As I remember it, the police called my house that night some time after eleven o'clock. I immediately called Mr. Tokura, the tennis coach. No doubt B was shocked to see him show up instead of me, his homeroom teacher and advisor. He asked Tokura why I hadn't come, and was apparently told that it was because I was "a woman." B took this to mean that my situation at home made it impossible for me to be there for him—he assumed that I hadn't come because I'm a single mother and my own child took priority over my students.

In the car, on the way back to B's home, Mr. Tokura apparently continued the criticism of B that he'd begun during tennis practice. "So the cram school teacher embarrassed you in front of the class and you went off to that game center. You worry too much about what other people think. When you get out of school, you're going to have to learn to put up with a lot worse than a little scolding." B's reaction—that the coach had verbally abused him—was typically childish, but I was impressed by the way Mr. Tokura sized up the situation and offered B the appropriate advice.

As he was telling his story there in the living room, B's mother had been sighing and murmuring sympathetically about the trials and tribulations of her "poor boy." I couldn't help being disgusted by her stupidity, but I also found myself becoming terribly jealous that she still had a child upon whom to pour all of this misplaced affection. At any rate, though B had been in some sense the victim in this incident, our school strictly forbids students to go to the game center under any circumstances. As punishment for his infraction, B was assigned to clean the pool deck and the changing room after school for a week.

At the beginning of February, A succeeded in tripling the voltage flowing to the zipper, and he was anxious to test it out. Around the same time, he noticed that B, who sat next to him in class, had been scribbling "Die! Die! Die!" in his notebook. He stopped B after school one day and asked whether he wanted to see a sex tape he'd managed to get hold of. B had heard about A's tapes and immediately agreed. Very soon after the two of them began spending time together, A asked whether B had anybody he wanted to "punish." B was naturally a bit puzzled, but A explained about his coin purse and the fact that he'd managed to increase its power. "I invented the thing to punish bad guys, so we need a bad guy to try it out on."

B knew about the purse, of course, and about A's success at the science fair. He'd been impressed, like everyone else in the class. But now that he was being given the chance to see how it worked, he mentioned the first name that came to mind: Mr. Tokura. A rejected the idea out of hand, however, showing what a coward he actually is. He would never act without hiding behind his inventions, and he refused to take on someone as strong as Tokura. B suggested me next— apparently out of lingering anger over my having sent his tennis coach to the police station instead of going myself. A rejected this idea, too—no doubt realizing that I wasn't likely to be fooled twice by his little toy. But even worse, he knew I wasn't going to make a fuss over it under any circumstances—which is, of course, exactly what he wanted.

At that point, B remembered that he'd seen Manami by the pool when he'd been cleaning the deck. "What about Moriguchi's daughter?" he asked, and finally A agreed. A knew that I had been bringing Manami to school on Wednesday afternoons. B added important details: that Manami was coming to the pool by herself to feed the dog; and that she had pestered me for a Snuggly Bunny pouch at the mall but that I'd refused to buy it for her. The mention of the pouch got A's attention.

The next Wednesday, when school had let out, A and B hid in the locker room by the pool and waited for Manami. They saw her come out on the pool deck, produce a piece of bread from under her jacket, and feed it to Muku through the fence. The boys approached her from behind, and B spoke first.

"Hello," he said. "You're Manami, aren't you? We're in your mother's class, and I ran into you at Happy Town the other day." Manami was cautious at first. A realized that she might be worried that they would tell me they'd seen her at the pool, and he spoke to her in a soothing voice.

"Do you like dogs? Well, so do we. That's why we come here sometimes, to feed the pup." When Manami heard that these big boys were coming to feed Muku, too, she relaxed and dropped her guard, and at that moment A produced the Snuggly Bunny pouch he'd had hidden behind his back. "Your momma didn't get this for you, did she? Or did she get it for you later?" Manami shook her head. "The truth is, she asked us to go and buy it for you. So here it is, an early Valentine present from your mother." A reached out and put the strap of the pouch around her neck, and Manami seemed elated at the gift. "Go ahead and open it," A added. "There's chocolate inside." At the instant her hand touched the zipper, Manami collapsed to the ground and lay motionless. A satisfied smile spread over A's face. B was in a state of shock, unable to believe what he'd just seen. "Gotcha!" he heard A whisper.

"What happened?" he said. His voice was breaking as he grabbed A's shoulder. "What have you done? She's not moving!"

"Then go and tell someone—tell everyone!" A said. He brushed B's hand aside and walked away with a satisfied look on his face.

Left alone, B became convinced that Manami was dead. But he was shaking with fear and couldn't bring himself to look at her body. He found himself staring instead into the eyes of Snuggly Bunny, whose head formed the fatal pouch. If they found out that this thing had killed her, then they'd find out he was an accomplice to murder. Averting his eyes, he pulled the pouch from Manami's neck and threw it over the fence, as far away as he could. Then he thought of a plan. He could make it look as though she'd fallen into the pool. He picked up Manami's body and threw it into the cold, dark water. Then he ran away as fast as his legs could carry him.

As he came to the end of his story, B added that he barely remembered the events he'd been describing due to the shock he had experienced at the time, but he felt that he'd been honest with me—that he'd told the truth.

So this was how Manami really died.

A and B continued to come to school, despite the fact that I now knew the truth. They saw no signs that the police were about to appear in our classroom. A wondered about this; in fact, when he'd finished his confession, with that almost ecstatic look on his face, he'd asked me as much. Why hadn't I reported my suspicions to the authorities? But I told him that nothing had changed, that it would still be regarded as an accident, and I had no intention of turning it into the kind of sensational murder he had wanted it to be. Then there was B's mother, who had listened to her son's confession with a blank, dumbfounded look on her face. I told her that as a mother myself I wanted to kill both A and B. But, I added, I am also a teacher, and though I recognized my duty to report these crimes and make sure they received the appropriate punishment, I had a teacher's duty to protect my students. Since the police had determined Manami's death to be an accident, I told her I had no intention of reopening the case and stirring up trouble. You can imagine that it was a rather noble little speech.

I went home, but a short time later there was a call from B's father, who had heard the whole story when he returned from work. He wanted to discuss some sort of monetary compensation, what they call a "solatium," but I wouldn't hear of it. If I took money from his family, B would feel that the whole thing had been put to rest. But I want him to reflect on what he's done and to lead a better life from here on, without ever forgetting his crime. And if his father finds it necessary to be around a bit more to support his son when his past is weighing heavily on him—well, all the better.

Now that is a reasonable question. How do I justify letting them go free when it's possible A might kill again?

You certainly have been paying attention—I suppose it's a skill you learn from your computer games. Though I have to admit it's hard for me to understand why you got so frantic when I was talking about HIV and can listen to the story of a murder without even getting upset. But you misunderstand when you worry about A killing "again." ... You see, he didn't kill Manami in the first place. B did. That night after Mrs. Takenaka left, I came back to school and measured the voltage in the pouch. Without going into the details, what I found was that the purse was incapable of stopping the heart of an old person with coronary disease, or even that of a four-year-old child. I tested it myself, and I can assure you that the shock was far less painful than the one I'd had from touching a frayed cord on my washing machine. I'm convinced that Manami was just unconscious. As I said earlier, the cause of Manami's death was drowning. The next day, when it was reported that she'd been found in the pool, A went to B and asked him why he'd butted in and done something so unnecessary. I suppose I wanted to ask B the same thing, though for different reasons. Even if he couldn't bring himself to go get help for her, why didn't he just run away?

If he had, Manami would still be alive!

I do not want to be a saint.

I am not being noble by keeping the identity of A and B a secret. I haven't told the police because I simply don't trust the law to punish them. A fully intended to kill Manami but didn't actually cause her death; while B had no desire to kill her but brought about her death. If I did hand them over to the police, they probably wouldn't even be sentenced to a juvenile institution; they'd be let out on probation and the whole thing would be forgotten. I wish I could electrocute A. Drown B like he did my daughter. But neither punishment would bring back

Manami. Nor would they be able to repent for their crimes if they were already dead. I wanted them to understand the value, the terrible weight, of human life, and once they'd understood, I wanted them to fully realize the consequences of what they had done—and to live with that realization. So how was I supposed to accomplish this?

I know someone who lives with this kind of weight on his shoulders. He provided me with some inspiration.

If you'll remember, this whole discussion started with the idea of calcium deficiency, but calcium isn't the only thing we lack. In the past, Japanese people had a refined sense of taste, but these days it's said that more and more children can't even tell the difference between hot and mild curry, a problem supposedly caused by a zinc deficiency. So, I wonder about all of you—how sensitive are your tongues? A and B, specifically—their tongues. It looks as though you all finished your milk, but did any of you notice an odd flavor? Perhaps a bit like iron? You see, I added some blood to the cartons that went to A and B this morning. Not my blood. The blood of the most noble man I know—Manami's father, Saint Sakuranomi.

I can see from your reactions that most of you have figured it out.

I'm not sure how quickly my little experiment will take effect, but I would like to urge A and B to have their blood tested in a few months. The incubation period for the HIV virus is usually between five and ten years, so that should give you plenty of time to think about the value of life. It's my hope that you'll come to understand what a terrible thing you've done, and that you'll beg forgiveness from Manami's spirit. As for the rest of you, you'll be continuing on together as a class next year, so I expect you to look out for these two and take special care of them. I doubt you'll be sending your new teacher any of those frivolous text messages about the value of living.

I haven't decided yet what I'll be doing next. The truth is, I may not have the freedom to decide after today. But if something is to happen to me, I only hope that it will be delayed long enough for me to see the results of what I've done.

What's that? What if the results never appear?

Well, then, I suggest A and B watch out for swerving cars.

I am hoping to spend spring break with Manami's father. We've been living together since the "accident," and though he doesn't have much time left, we have decided to spend it peacefully together. I hope you have a productive and pleasant vacation, and I want to thank you for the past year.

Class is dismissed.

CHAPTER TWO

The Martyr

Just a few months ago I saw you every day, Yūko-sensei, but now I don't know how to find you or where to send this letter. You stood there in front of us and told us that you couldn't trust the law to punish the boys who had taken the life of your little girl, that you were going to handle them yourself—and then you disappeared. That was pretty thoughtless, I think. If you were going to do that to them, then you should at least stay and face the consequences. You should be here to see what happens to them.

I decided you need to know the rest of the story, what happened after you left us, and so I tried writing you a long letter to tell you everything. Then I realized I didn't know where to mail it or what to do with it—until I remembered a new writers' prize they were advertising in that magazine you were always reading in the teachers' lounge. Kids in their teens win those things all the time, so I decided to send my letter in to the contest. It's a long shot, but who knows—

One thing worries me, though. The magazine had been running a column by Sakuranomi-sensei for months now, but it ended in April. So even if I win the contest and they print my letter, you may have stopped reading it. Like I said—a long shot.

Anyway, I want you to understand that I'm not doing this because I want your help. It's just that there's something I've got to ask you.

It's this: Can you feel it in the air? Do you sense it in the atmosphere? Whether it's stale or fresh, stagnant or fluid? I'm convinced that the auras of all the people in any place get together to create the mood. I guess I'm supersensitive to this kind of stuff—probably because I never got comfortable with my own aura. Sometimes I feel like I can't breathe, and all I can think about is the feeling of the air around me.

Anyway, if you had to pick a word to describe the air in our class after the new teacher came, you'd have to say it was...bizarre.

We haven't seen Naoki since that day you left, when you told us what you'd done to him and Shūya. But he was the only one absent in B Class on the first day of the new school year. Everybody else was there, even Shūya. I guess that was actually more surprising—that he was there. Nobody said anything to him, we just stood around whispering about him. And he didn't seem to care at all. He sat down at his desk and started reading some book, but there was a cover on it so I couldn't tell what it was. Not that he was acting tough or anything—that's what he's done every day since we started middle school. But that's what was so weird: Nothing seemed to have changed.

It was nice out and the windows were wide open, but the air in the classroom seemed heavy and stale. Then the first bell rang and our new homeroom teacher came in. He's young and kind of bouncy or something, and he went right up to the blackboard and wrote his name.

"They've been calling me Werther ever since I was in school, so that's what I want you to call me, too." We still feel pretty weird about it, but that's what I'll call him here. "But don't worry," he told us, "the name's the same, but that doesn't mean I've got the Sorrows part." Nobody laughed.

"What? You haven't read it?" he said, moaning and striking this dumb pose like he was in a play or something. Of course we got it: The characters for his name in Japanese mean "worthy," so some nerd figured out that was "Werther" in German and thought it would be cute to pretend he was the guy from *The Sorrows of Young Werther*. We got it. Very funny. But didn't he get it? Couldn't he tell what was going on in the room? Didn't he feel the air?

"Oops, almost forgot. We need to call roll. So I know Naoki's absent—his mom called to say he has a cold—but is everybody else here?" Another bad sign: He was already trying to buddy up to us, calling us by our first names. You never did do that; you always treated us with respect. Then he started right in with his self-introduction.

"I wasn't much of a student in middle school myself," he said. "I smoked, and if a teacher got on my bad side, I'd let the air out of his tires or something. But my homeroom teacher for eighth grade straightened me out. He was the type of guy who would toss out his whole lesson plan when something had happened to one of his students, when he felt like there was something serious that needed talking about — and I bet we missed at least five English classes just for my little crises!" He laughed at this point, but I doubt anyone was actually listening to him. They were probably all thinking, like I was, about Naoki's "cold."

We all knew he wasn't sick — not in the way Werther thought, anyway. But I guess I was a little relieved to hear that he was still planning to come to school — that he hadn't transferred somewhere else. A lot of kids were glancing around at Shūya through all of this, but he just sat there looking at the teacher like some honor student — though you could tell he wasn't really listening, either. Werther didn't seem to notice one way or the other and just charged on.

"This is the first day of my first teaching job, so you, members of B Class, are my first-ever students! And since I'm new, I want you to be able to start fresh, too, so I've decided that I'm not even going to read the files your first-year homeroom teacher left on each of you. I want you to feel like this is a new beginning, and I want you to think of me as a big brother, as someone you can talk to about anything at all."

They always extend homeroom that first day before the opening ceremony, and Werther had talked for what seemed like forever. But finally he wound things up by taking out this brand-new piece of yellow chalk and writing on the board in huge letters:

ONE FOR ALL! ALL FOR ONE!

I don't really know what you thought of us—as individuals, I mean. And I can't imagine what you might have written about Naoki and Shūya in those files. But if Werther had bothered to read them, I bet none of this would have happened.

Naoki was absent day after day, and none of us said a word to Shūya, but things were pretty calm going into the middle of May. It wasn't like we were all being mean to Shūya or hated him or anything—more like everyone had just decided that he didn't even exist. We all got really good at avoiding him, just like we got used to ignoring the stifling feeling in the classroom.

One night they played this show on TV that was about a middle school, and they mentioned that some class had decided to use the homeroom period as reading time. They said that just those ten minutes a day had improved the students' attitude and helped with their ability to focus, and that the kids actually improved academically. As I was watching, I thought about Shūya.

The next day, there was a new "library" in the back of the homeroom class. Werther had brought this little bookshelf and a whole bunch of books from home.

"I know they're a little dog-eared, but I want us all to start reading every morning and getting absolutely everything we can out of life!" Werther told us. Like everything he said, this sounded pretty dorky, but it didn't seem like a bad idea...until we went to look at the titles of the books. I have to tell you that most of us had started to get used to Werther by this point— maybe even liked him a little. He is pretty good-looking, after all. But after that we could never take him seriously again. You see, one whole shelf of the case was filled with books by your friend Sakuranomi-sensei, Manami's father.

I guess Werther couldn't help noticing that we weren't impressed with his little library. Maybe that's why he took a book off the shelf when we were doing problems in his math class later in the day and started reading to us.

"...I was never interested in religion, but as I wandered around the world, going from country to country, somehow I started carrying the Bible with me. There's a verse in Matthew 18 that talks about a man who has a hundred sheep. Now if one of those sheep is lost, the man will leave the ninety-nine on the mountain and go looking for the one; and if he finds it, he'll take more pleasure in the sheep that was lost than in the rest that did not go astray. Now to me, that's the definition of a true teacher..." At that point, he closed the book. "Let's forget about math for today and have a class meeting," he said, his voice getting really quiet and almost churchlike or something. "I wonder if we can't put our heads together and think what to do about Naoki." I guess he suddenly realized that Naoki was a lost sheep. Anyway, he had us put away our math books without even checking the answers to the problems.

Naoki had a "cold" for the first week of school, but after that Werther had just said that he "wasn't feeling well."

"I have to admit that I've been lying to you about the reason Naoki hasn't been coming to school. He isn't playing hooky. He wants to be here, but somehow he lacks the will to come—it's a psychological block of some kind."

I couldn't really see what the difference was between "wanting to come" and "having the will to come," but that's the spin Werther put on it—though it wasn't clear whether the explanation was his own idea or he was just repeating what Naoki's mother had said.

"I apologize for not being honest with you about this," Werther said, and I guess I felt a little sorry for him just then. Naoki had a psychological block all right, but Werther was the only one in the room who didn't know how he got it.

I don't think anyone in the class told anyone else about the things you said before you left. After school that day, we all got the same text—"If you tell what A and B did, you're C"—though we never did figure out who sent it.

All this was leading up to Werther's big idea: "I want us to think about how we can create an environment that will make it easier for Naoki to come to school," he told us.

Of course, nobody said anything to this. Even Kenta, who had been playing the straight man for a lot of Werther's stupid jokes, just sat staring down at his desk. But Werther chose not to notice—or to assume that we were all thinking hard about what he'd said—and started in, telling us his own ideas. As usual, I doubt he really cared what we were thinking anyway.

"Why don't we make copies of your class notes and deliver them to Naoki at home?" This brought disgusted groans from various places around the room. "Why not?" Werther asked Ryōji, picking on him because his groan had been the loudest.

"Because," Ryōji muttered, not looking up, "my house is on the other side of town from his." Not bad for an on-the-fly excuse.

"No worries," said Werther. "How 'bout we do this? You take notes in shifts, and then once a week Mizuki and I will deliver them to Naoki's house."

Why me? Because I'm class president again this year (Yūsuke's vice president, by the way), and because I live in the same neighborhood as Naoki. I made sure not to let on how I felt about his plan, but I guess he could tell I wasn't thrilled right from the start. At one point he asked me straight out why I was cold with him—I don't know for sure why he would say that, but it might be because I was the only one who refused to call him Werther to his face. Anyway, the next thing I knew he was asking me whether *I* had a nickname. I told him I didn't—that everyone called me Mizuki—but then Ayako spoke up and practically shouted, "Mizuho!" And she was right, that was what everybody called me for the first few years of elementary school. "Mi-zu-*ho*," they'd say, stretching out the last syllable for emphasis.

"I *like* it!" Werther said. "It's settled. From now on I'm going to call you Mizuho. What about the rest of you? Fate brought all of us together in this class. Let's really get to know each other, break down all the walls between us!"

So after that, thanks to Werther, I went back to being Mizuho.

We started taking the notes to Naoki's house on the second Friday in May. I knew right where he lived and had actually been inside lots of times, since one of his older sisters had sort of taken care of me when I was six or seven.

Naoki's mom came to meet us at the door. I hadn't seen her in a long time, but she looked just the same—perfect makeup, beautiful clothes. When I'd been there playing with his sister, I remember how she would talk nonstop about Naoki, even when he wasn't in the room: how she was serving pancakes because they're his favorite, how he'd found her crying from cutting onions one day and had handed her his little handkerchief, how he'd taken third in the handwriting contest.

I thought we'd just give her the class notes and leave, but we ended up going in and sitting down in the living room. Naoki's mom didn't seem too thrilled about this, but Werther had apparently been planning on it from the beginning.

I knew the living room, too. I used to play Othello there with his sister. Naoki's room was right over where we played, and his mother would call up toward the ceiling and tell him to bring down a deck of cards. The sister who took care of me then is off at college in Tokyo now, and there was no way to tell whether Naoki was up there. His mother served us tea and then sat down to talk to Werther.

"Your predecessor is responsible for Naoki's emotional difficulties," she said. "If every teacher were as dedicated and enthusiastic as you clearly are, this would never have happened."

As I watched her, I knew Naoki hadn't told her what you'd said and done to him that last day in class. If he had, she wouldn't have been so full of herself, and she couldn't have sat there bad-mouthing you. Since he hadn't told her, that meant he was suffering up there all by himself. Anyway, she went on complaining about you—Moriguchi this and Moriguchi that—without mentioning what happened to your daughter. I doubt she even knew that Naoki had been involved.

Naoki never came down, and eventually I realized we were only there to listen to her griping. But Werther sat nodding with this stupid, sympathetic look on his face, as if this was the most wonderful thing he'd ever heard. I'm not sure he was even listening to her.

"Ma'am," he said, when she finally paused. "I want you to leave Naoki's problems to me!" There was a noise from upstairs just then, and I looked up at the ceiling again. Naoki must have heard everything.

Still, he didn't show up for school the next day, or the day after that. On the other hand, that seemed natural enough to us—as natural as the fact that we were all pretending Shūya wasn't there, even though he was. It seemed the best solution at the time.

They started handing out milk again on the first Monday in June. The Health Ministry had published the results of the pilot program "Promoting Dairy Products to the Nation's

Secondary Students"—"Milk Time"—and the prefecture had decided to follow up with a program of its own.

As class officers, Yūsuke and I had the job of handing out the cartons, but as we made our way around the room, we could feel the air getting heavier, feel the bad memories coming back. Fortunately, no one *had* to drink the milk. The prefecture had made the case for the benefits, but plenty of parents had complained that their children didn't like milk or were allergic to it. I'm amazed that there are so many moms and dads willing to spoil their kids like that, but that day it meant that there were no names on the cartons and that we were free to drink or not—and when you looked around, the only person in the room sucking on a straw was Werther himself.

"Hey, hey! What's the matter? Don't you know milk's good for you?" He finished the last drops and crushed the carton. Yumi made the mistake of looking up and catching his eye.

"I'm taking mine home," she murmured.

"Great idea!" Werther laughed. "A pick-me-up for when you need it." He watched as we all put our milk in our bags.

Shūya had classroom cleanup duty that afternoon. Just as he was turning around to get the broom out of the closet, there was the sound of something splattering. Yūsuke had thrown his milk carton at him, and his aim was perfect. It had exploded all over Shūya's back. I was sitting at my desk working on the class log, and I didn't realize what had happened at first. There were just a few kids still in the room, but every one of them was staring at Yūsuke.

I don't know how they really felt about Shūya, but even if they hated his guts, none of them would have had the courage to do something like that. Courage? I'm not sure that's the right word. But I guess it felt like courage, coming from an athletic, outgoing kid like Yūsuke. Shūya hadn't turned around when Yūsuke spoke up.

"You aren't even sorry, are you?"

But that didn't get a look out of Shūya, either. He glanced down at the milk all over his pants, picked up his bag, and walked out of the room. We just watched him go in silence.

That was the beginning of Shūya's punishment.

I think Yūsuke must have liked you a lot.

I realize now that you weren't the kind of teacher who makes a fuss over her students. You were more interested in finding the real value in each individual. You never made a big deal about it, but you always noticed when someone got the top score on a test, or did something great for her club, or got elected to school office.... You would announce it before homeroom or science class and make sure we gave them a round of applause.

You had them clap for me more than once in homeroom. The "class president" is really just the class maid, someone who never gets noticed or thanked, but you made a point of telling everyone I was doing a good job and asking them to show their appreciation. It was awkward, standing up there, but it still felt good.

Werther, on the other hand, never does anything like that. He's always talking about "only one" or "number one"—

some song he's obsessed with. When they introduced the new teachers at the assembly on the first day of school, he even sang part of it when it was his turn to speak.

"I don't want to focus only on the best students or the top athletes. I want to value each individual for the effort he brings to everything he does. I want to be a teacher who can view each student fairly."

At the beginning of May, our baseball team beat this private school that usually wins the whole league, and they made it all the way to the semifinals. It was a first for the school and the local paper even had an article, with pictures of the team—and to top it all off, the hero of the game, the ace of the pitching staff, was our own Yūsuke. After the tournament, he was named to the all-star team and interviewed for another article in the paper. Everybody was totally in awe (with the possible exception of Shūya), and for the first time since the start of the school year the classroom didn't seem like a funeral home. But leave it to Werther to screw things up.

Despite everything he'd said about wanting to treat everybody the same, he didn't seem to care about anybody but "number one." He made a really big deal out of Yūsuke and ignored everybody else. If you'd been here, I know you would have praised Yūsuke, too, but I'm sure you would have pointed out that he hadn't won the game alone, that baseball's a team sport and no matter how good the pitcher is, he can't play the game alone. You would have had us applaud the whole team. Why couldn't Werther have done that?

I don't think they realized it at the time, but I'll bet Yūsuke and every kid in class you ever singled out felt there was something missing in the way Werther handled things. You could feel the frustration and anger in the room, feel that kids needed a way to let it out. But no one took it out on Shūya— at least not yet.

I was going with Werther every Friday to visit Naoki's house. That first day, his mother had sat us down in the living room so she could complain about you, but after that, when we kept coming back, she cut the visits shorter and shorter and kept us standing in the entrance hall. Finally, she stopped letting us in or even undoing the chain. She just took the envelope through a crack in the door. I could tell from the glimpses I got as we talked with her that she was still taking time with her makeup, but I thought her lips looked a little swollen.

Naoki's oldest sister had married and moved to Tokyo, and his father usually got home late from work, so much of the time it was just Naoki and his mother—and he was living with a terrible secret.

I told Werther that I didn't think we'd get to see Naoki no matter how many times we went to visit, and that it actually seemed like we were stalking him or something. For one second he got this nasty look on his face, but then he forced another smile.

"No, Mizuho," he said, "we're just getting to the critical point for both of us. If we can hold on a little longer, I'm sure they'll understand what we're trying to do." It was clear he wasn't going to give up on the visits, but I wasn't sure who he meant by "both of us" or the "critical point." I wasn't even sure Werther had ever met Naoki, since he hadn't come to school once this year. But it seemed too late to be asking about that now.

The next Monday Werther showed up for math class with a piece of white cardboard and said he wanted us to write messages to Naoki to "buck him up" and get him to come back to school. I knew the room's aura was in for a change, but it wasn't exactly what I expected. As they worked on the "get-well card" for Naoki, some of the girls were giggling and a few boys even laughed. I had no idea why, but when it reached me, the board was nearly filled up with a line of odd phrases:

Don't worry! Imagine happiness! Everyone wins! Maybe you too? Unless you don't? Remember everything! Don't ever forget! Everyone knows! Really we do! Everyone knows! Remember!

Only now, as I'm writing this, can I see what they were doing. How could I have been so stupid? But they sure seemed to be enjoying themselves as they worked.

Do you remember that you told us about the Juvenile Law that day? Even though it's meant to protect kids, I already had my doubts about it before hearing what you had to say.

What about that case in H City where that boy killed a woman and her baby? I remember seeing her relatives talking about them on TV for days, about how senseless it was, how happy they'd been in life, how brutal the boy who killed them had been. I remember thinking then that you really didn't need a trial in a case like that. You could just hand the criminal over to the victim's family and let them do what they wanted with him. The people who are hurt most should have the right to judge the ones who hurt them, the way you did with Naoki and Shūya, and you'd only need a trial when no one was left behind. But it wasn't just that evil boy who bothered me. I couldn't stand the lawyers, the way they stood up there and said everything they could think of to defend the kid. Anybody could tell they were lying. I'm sure there's a reason they have all those laws, and I know they have to stand up there arguing like that and looking important, but when you see them on TV you can't help thinking you'd like to have them right there in the room with you so you could give them what they had coming. Or maybe if you could just find out where they live and go throw a few rocks through their windows. At least that's how I feel.

And that's in a case where I don't even know the victims or their family. Something I've only seen on TV — something that happened far away. But if I feel that way, I'm sure a lot of other people do, too. . . .

But as I've been writing this to you, I've changed my mind. I've realized that you have to have a trial, no matter how terrible the crime is. Not for the criminal but for the average people, to make sure they understand what's happened and to keep them from taking the law into their own hands.

I suppose everybody wants to be recognized for what they've done; everybody wants to be praised. But doing something good or remarkable isn't easy. It's much easier to condemn people who do the wrong thing than it is to do the right thing yourself. But even then, it takes a certain amount of courage to be the *first* one to come out and blame someone else. What if no one else joins you? No one else stands up to condemn the wrongdoer? On the other hand, it's easy to join in condemning someone once someone else has gotten the ball rolling. You don't even have to put yourself out there; all you have to do is say, "Me, too!"

It doesn't end there: You also get the benefit of feeling that you're doing good by picking on someone evil—it can even be a kind of stress release. Once you've done it, though, you may find that you want that feeling again—that you need someone else to accuse just to get the rush back. You may have started with real bad guys, but the second time around you may have to look further down the food chain, be more and more creative in your charges and accusations.

And at that point you're pretty much conducting a witch hunt—just like in the Middle Ages. I think we regular people may have forgotten a basic truth—we don't really have the right to judge anyone else.

After that day when Yūsuke hit Shūya in the back, there were almost always milk cartons shoved in Shūya's desk. The worst was when somebody kept one for a week or more and the milk turned sour, or when there were too many and they broke open. They put them in his shoe cubby and his locker, too. But Shūya just cleared them all away without a word, as though it was just part of his morning routine. His notebooks and gym clothes disappeared a lot, and someone wrote

"Murderer" on every page of one of his textbooks. Most of us were still ignoring him, but a few mixed-up kids harassed him nonstop.

But one day we all got the same text on our phones: "You be the Judge! Collect points for every blow you strike against Shūya the Killer!"

It came from the same person who sent the text after you talked to us. The system was simple: Every time you did something to harass Shūya, you'd send details to the original sender and he would award you points. He'd total up the score on Saturday, and the person with the fewest points would be labeled "Friend of the Killer," and he'd get the same treatment as Shūya starting on the following Monday.

You know I didn't feel any sympathy for Shūya, but this just seemed totally dumb, so I decided right away that I was going to ignore the whole thing. And I was pretty sure a lot of other kids would do the same. But a few days later I happened to spot two of the quietest girls in the class, Yukari and Satsuki (you know them...their idea of excitement is an Art Club meeting), standing near the shoe cupboards, sending a text—and then I realized they were reporting that they'd just stuffed their milk cartons in with Shūya's shoes.

If those two were playing the game, I'd be the only one who ended up with no points at all.

So I was a little nervous when I headed to school the following Monday, but the day passed without anything unusual happening. Apparently, some other kids had refused to join in—had decided not to score points off Shūya. Maybe the world wasn't going crazy after all.

*   *   *

One day toward the end of June, Werther canceled math to hold a class meeting, even though exams were just a few days off. He told us he had something he wanted to talk about, and then he started waving this piece of paper at us.

"I found this in one of your homework notebooks," he said. We could hear the kids in the front row kind of gulp, but from where I was sitting you couldn't see anything.

"There are bullies in this class!" he said in this really dramatic voice, reading the words off the paper. I have to admit I was pretty impressed by the courage it had taken to write this—and it meant that somebody else wanted things to change, too. But I also realized that whoever wrote it had probably not thought it would be read out in front of the whole class like this. He—or she—was probably sweating it out about now.

"I'm not going to say whose notebook it was in," Werther continued, looking around the room, "but I want us to discuss this problem as a class right now. I can tell, you know, I've been feeling that something's not quite right. It's not right when a good student like Shūya is telling me for the third time this month that he's 'lost his notebook' and has to get a new one. And it's not just his notebooks—he's 'lost' his gym clothes and his shoes, too. So I was just about to ask Shūya what's going on. But before I got the chance, some brave soul sent me this message asking for help...and I can't tell you how happy that makes me. But I have to say that what's going on here can't be called bullying. This sort of harassment isn't bullying—it's jealousy, plain and simple. The proof is that no one has dared to attack him directly; it's just this constant messing with his things. Shūya is one of the best students in the whole grade, and I'm told he won an award in a national science competition last year. So it's pretty natural that some of you are jealous of him and that you might even go so far as to harass him because of it. Which is why I have no intention of trying to find out who did this. It's your problem as a class.

"But I do have something to say to you—whether you've been involved in this or not. It's clear that Shūya is a very bright student, but that doesn't mean that he's better than the rest of you in any way. Being a good student and getting good grades is what *Shūya* does well—it's his own special gift. But each of you has his or her gift as well, and rather than worrying about Shūya, I want you to find that gift and spend some time developing it. I'm sure some of you have no idea what it might be, and if that's the case I urge you to come see me. It's only been a few months since we've met, but I've been watching you carefully, and I think I've got some ideas...."

Just at that moment, the text tone went off on a phone, and Takahiro stuck his hand in his desk to kill the battery. "Shit," he muttered. Having the phone wasn't a problem, but we're supposed to turn them off in class. Werther took the phone and then went on with his speech.

"This is serious stuff I'm trying to talk about," he said. "But one joker who can't play by the rules can interrupt the whole thing. Turn them off! Any first grader knows that!"

The sermon went on for a while after that, but it seemed

like getting interrupted by Takahiro was a bigger deal than the bullying. So if the writer of that note had really been looking for help from Werther, he must have been sighing under his breath by then.

But the real nightmare hadn't even started yet. The witch trials were about to begin.

It didn't take long—in fact, it was that same day after school. I haven't joined any clubs this year, but I did stay late to take my turn cleaning the classroom. I was just about to get my shoes out of the cupboard at the front door when Maki stopped me. Nothing has changed with Maki since you left: She's still Ayako's sidekick and gopher.

"Ayako has something she wants to see you about," she said. "Can you come back to the room?"

I was pretty sure the "something" wasn't going to be pleasant, but if I refused I'd just have to deal with it later, so I followed her back to the class. As I walked through the door, Maki shoved me from behind and I went down on my knees. When I looked up, Ayako was standing there. Then I realized that there were five or six kids forming a circle around me.

"You blabbed to Werther, didn't you, Mizuho?" Ayako said. She was completely wrong, but I'd thought that something like this might be coming.

"No," I said, staring back at her. "It wasn't me."

"Liar!" she barked. "It couldn't be anybody else. But you are so wrong! What did you mean, 'bullying'? That's total crap! What we're doing here is punishing a killer. Don't you have any sympathy for Moriguchi-sensei? Or are you sweet on that murderer?"

There was no sense trying to reason with her, so I just shook my head, rejecting everything she'd said.

"So you're not sweet on him? Well, prove it then," she said, holding out a milk carton. "Hit him with this and we'll believe you."

As I took the carton from Ayako, I suddenly noticed Shūya lying on the floor on the other side of the room, his arms and legs bound with tape. Ayako and the rest of them turned to look at him with these nasty grins on their faces.

If I didn't throw the milk at him, I knew I'd be getting the same treatment tomorrow—or, worse yet, they would probably start doing all the stuff to me they were too scared to do to Shūya.

Then our eyes met. I couldn't really tell what he was thinking, but I knew Shūya's eyes weren't pleading with me or trying to make me mad—they just looked really calm. As I stared into his eyes, I suddenly understood: He wasn't thinking about anything, wasn't feeling anything at all. He was the perfect image of a heartless killer. I know you said that Naoki was the one who actually killed Manami, but if Shūya hadn't been there, none of this would have happened!

Murderer! Murderer! Murderer! Suddenly I had no more doubts.

I got up and took a few steps toward him. Then I aimed at his chest, shut my eyes, and threw the carton as hard as I could. I could hear it bursting, and at that instant, I felt this weird kind of ecstasy come up from somewhere deep inside me.

I want to hurt this bastard! I want to make him pay! I want to make him taste his own medicine! Stuff like that went through me like an electric current, round and round in my head... until it was finally stopped by the sound of the kids laughing. What was so funny? As I opened my eyes, I could see. Milk was dripping down Shūya's face, and a red spot was swelling on his cheek. I'd missed his chest, but I'd hit him right in the face.

"Nice, Mizuho!" Ayako muttered, and they laughed even harder. But I couldn't understand what they found so funny—not while Shūya was still staring at me with those eyes. And now I thought I knew what they were saying.

Do you really have the right to judge me? He suddenly seemed to me like some sort of saint, persecuted by the mindless horde.

"I'm sorry," I blurted out, and I knew right away that Ayako had heard me.

"Wait a *minute!*" she shouted. "Did I just hear you *apologize* to this killer? Mizuho's no better than he is! Let's give her what she has coming!" Ayako can get really dramatic, like she's channeling Joan of Arc or something... though I doubt she's ever heard of her.

In a flash they had my arms pinned behind my back. I knew it was one of the boys in our class who grabbed me, but I'm not sure who. It hurt. I was scared. I wanted somebody to help me—that's about all that was running through my head.

"From this day forward!"—Ayako was still putting on a show—"You and this boy are one!" Then they pushed me to the floor, and I came to rest with my face just a few inches from Shūya's.

"Kiss! Kiss! Kiss!" They started to clap and chant. I wanted to yell at them to stop, but I was frozen with fear. The boy who was pinning my arms took hold of the back of my head with his other hand and pressed forward until my face met Shūya's and I heard a clicking sound.

"Look, Ayako, I got it!" As Maki spoke, my arms were released and I turned to find the whole group gathered around her to look at her phone. They were still laughing.

"Was that your first kiss, Mizuho?" Ayako said, taking the phone from Maki and shoving it in my face. The picture on the screen showed Shūya and me with our lips pressed together. "Now what we do with this is up to you, Mizuho," she said.

Moriguchi-sensei, I know that Naoki and Shūya are murderers, but that doesn't mean I can forgive kids who would do something like this.

I don't really remember how I got home that afternoon. My clothes smelled like milk, so I got out of them and took a shower. Then I shut myself in my room and didn't come out for dinner.

I had a vague feeling that someone was still holding my arms behind my back, and the sound of laughter rang in my ears. I couldn't stop shaking. I wanted the night to last forever, or for a nuclear missile to come and annihilate everything—and I couldn't even sleep because the whole horrible scene came back to me the minute I closed my eyes.

Around midnight I heard a text coming to my phone. I was afraid they might be sending me the picture, but when I looked, it was a number I hardly recognized: Shūya's. He wanted to know whether I'd meet him at a convenience store nearby. I thought about it for a minute and then decided to go.

Shūya was standing next to his bicycle at the edge of the parking lot. I had no idea what to say or even how to look at him, so I stood facing him over the bike. Without a word, he reached into the pocket of his jeans, fished out a piece of paper, unfolded it, and held it up. The streetlights were pretty bright, but I still couldn't see what it was. I had to strain my eyes, but finally I could tell it was some numbers, and with a little more effort I saw that it was the results of a blood test—with his name written at the top and a date from last week.

"It was in the mailbox when I got home," he said, folding the paper and putting it back in his pocket.

"I knew," I said.

He stared back at me with a surprised look on his face—not the look of a child killer but a look full of feeling, one I hadn't seen in a long time.

"There's something I've been wanting to tell you," I said. He went over to a vending machine and bought two cans of juice. Then he put them in the basket of the bicycle and told me to get on the back. Even an empty parking lot in the middle of the night was too public for what we had to talk about.

*   *   *

I wondered what we looked like riding double on the bike through the dark town. Not that there was anyone to see— we passed almost no people or cars—but I was a little nervous, even though there was nothing between us.

His back was broader than I thought—I'd assumed he'd been losing weight. As we rode through the dark, it seemed as though he'd arrived to rescue me, just as the world was coming to an end. But if he'd appeared out of the night to save me, then I had to tell him.

After we'd been riding for about fifteen minutes, the buildings began to thin out and he pulled up in front of a one-story house next to the river. It looked empty and I was pretty sure he didn't live here, but he got off the bike, produced a key, and opened the door. He must have been able to tell I was hesitating, because he turned around to explain that it had belonged to his grandmother and that his parents were using it to store stuff for their shop now that she was gone.

Once we were inside, he turned on the light and I could see piles of boxes lining the hallway. They must have blocked the breeze from getting in, because the air was heavy and humid, so we decided to sit down on the entrance step just inside the door. He gave me a can of grapefruit juice and I rolled it between my hands as I started to tell him what I'd done that day.

The day when you told us about Naoki and Shūya, there was just one part of the story I couldn't really believe—the ending. It was the scariest part, of course, and it was you, Moriguchi-sensei, I was afraid of.

After you left, Naoki ran out of the room and everybody else followed him. I was just about to leave, too, when I noticed the box by the blackboard with all the empty milk cartons lined up in the slots with our names. My first thought—the class president reflex—was to wonder who was on cleanup duty, but then I realized no one would want to touch the cartons, which was when I found myself looking for Naoki's and Shūya's.

You'd been talking a lot about looking at things logically that day, so maybe that's why I found myself wondering about *your* logic. I could sort of understand the pain and sadness you must have been feeling, but I knew I couldn't really know how you felt. I've got people I love just like anybody else, but they're all alive, and even if I try imagining how I'd feel if they died, it's still only imagining. But I was pretty sure that you would have some ability to be rational no matter how much you hated Naoki and Shūya.

That day I found a plastic bag in the cleaning cupboard and wrapped up the two cartons to take home. I realized I couldn't leave the box with just Naoki and Shūya's missing, so I took the rest of the cartons to the garbage bin behind the gym. I ran into a couple of teachers on the way, but they didn't say anything. Why would they suspect the class president when she was taking out the garbage? When I got home, I cut open the cartons and tested the milk left in them with a chemical that reacts with blood (strange, I know, but I had some on hand).

The results were just what I'd expected.

*　*　*

"Thanks for not telling anybody," Shūya said when I finished my story.

I didn't know what to say. I hadn't kept this a secret for his sake—I just didn't have a really close friend I could tell. But he was right: If I'd told anyone in our class, the attacks on him would have been even worse.

"But you believed everything else Moriguchi said?" he asked. I nodded. "And you're not afraid to be alone with me here?" This time I shook my head. "You don't mind talking to a child killer?"

I looked him in the eye. If he was a child killer, then what were the other kids in the class, the ones who had treated him like an animal? I was more afraid of myself for having thrown the milk at him than I was of Shūya. His cheek was still a little swollen. "I'm sorry," I said, reaching out to touch the red spot. Some part of me wanted to make myself feel what I'd done. The warmth of his skin sent a jolt through my body.

I don't think the shock was because I'd been holding the cold can or because his cheek was hot from the swelling. I realized I'd been thinking he was a bloodless demon, but the moment I touched him I knew he was just a boy like any other.

"Why did you show me the test results?" This is what I'd been wanting to ask him.

"Because I think we're a lot alike," he said.

I put my finger on the pull-tab on the can and looked at him, not knowing what to say. So he hadn't come out of the night to save me.

"Hold on," he said. "Are you really going to drink all that?"

I looked at the can. I could have drank the whole thing, but I thought I understood what he meant—and I realized I was glad. "No, I don't think I can," I told him. Then I put down my can and he handed me his. It was still half full, and I took a few sips before I handed it back to him. He drank some and then handed it back to me—and when the can was empty we kissed a while. I haven't told you, sensei, that there's actually somebody else I like, but this was different. At that moment I felt like Shūya was the only one in the world on my side.

He took me back to the convenience store, and then as we were saying good-bye he told me I had to come to school the next day. I really didn't want to go, but I was afraid if I didn't I would end up locking myself in at home for the rest of my life. And now, with Shūya there, I felt as though I could stand the cruelty.

"I'll be there," I promised him.

The moment I walked in the door the next morning some of the boys started to whistle, and I heard giggling from girls who were looking up at the blackboard. Someone had drawn a heart on the board and written my name and Shūya's in it. I kept my head down, the way Shūya always did, and went straight to my desk, but someone had drawn the same heart on the lid in permanent marker.

"Mizuho! Good morning!" It was Ayako, waving her phone at me from her desk, but I ignored her and opened the book I'd brought along.

It was the same way when Shūya arrived. He got the same

welcome, and he looked over at the blackboard, too. He had that same blank look as always, but when he got to his desk—which also had the heart—he put down his bag and walked over to Takahiro, who was still whistling.

"You got something you want to say, kid killer?" Takahiro said, grinning at Shūya. Shūya didn't answer. He just gave him this look and then he bit the tip of his little finger and ran it down Takahiro's cheek. It was like this symbolic line—a line of Shūya's blood—marking the end of punishment and the start of his counterattack. Some of the kids sitting nearby screamed, but then the room went completely quiet.

"You were the one holding down Mizuki, weren't you?" Shūya murmured close to Takahiro's ear. "Were you sucking up to *her?*" he added, looking over at Ayako. Then he walked over to her and held up his hand. A trickle of blood ran from his finger to his wrist. Ayako had covered her face with her hands, but Shūya reached down and picked up her phone in his bloody palm. She screamed.

"You act like a big shot," he said, "and get everybody else to do your dirty work, but you're too stupid to see that someone's playing you exactly the same way."

When he'd said this, he went and stood in front of Yūsuke, who had been watching from his desk in the back of the room as though none of this had anything to do with him.

"And that would be you, asshole, the one pulling her strings. You've been getting her to come after me." And then he bent down and kissed Yūsuke on the lips. Everyone in the room froze, and Yūsuke looked like he was going to be sick. "Did you like that?" Shūya asked, a big smile breaking out on his face. "You act all noble and talk about justice, but you knew Moriguchi's daughter was going to the pool. If you'd told somebody, she'd probably still be alive. This is all because you're feeling guilty, isn't it? Did it make you feel better messing with me? They've got a name for people like you. They're called hypocrites. Consider this your first and last warning—if you keep this up, the next kiss will have a lot of tongue."

After that no one bothered Shūya anymore.

In July, even after final exams had started, Shūya and I met at that house almost every day. I told my parents I was going to study with a friend, and since I've never given them any trouble, they didn't say anything even if I was a little late getting home. Shūya said his dad had remarried when he was in fifth grade and they had a new baby at home, so he used his grandmother's house to study in, and they barely seemed to notice if he didn't come home for a whole week at a time.

There was a room at the very back that Shūya calls his "laboratory." He didn't seem to be studying for exams. Instead he was working on an invention that looked a lot like a wristwatch, but when I asked him what it was, he refused to tell me. Still, I kind of liked sitting there watching him work on whatever it was. He finished it in the middle of July, and that was when he first told me it was a lie detector. He said there were sensors in the strap that could detect variations in the wearer's pulse. When something changed, the dial would light up and an alarm would go off.

"Try it," he told me.

I put it on my wrist, but I was pretty scared. What if it shocked me?

"Are you worried about getting shocked?" he asked, as though reading my mind.

"No, not really," I said.

Beep, beep, beep, beep...the face of the lie detector flashed, and it rang like a cheap alarm clock.

"It worked!" Shūya crowed. "Fantastic!"

"Fantastic," I repeated after him, actually feeling pretty impressed. This seemed to embarrass Shūya. He laughed. Then he grabbed my wrist and pulled it toward him.

"That's all I really wanted," he said. "Just somebody to notice me."

I realized he was talking about what had happened with Manami. It was the first time he'd said anything about it. I lay my free hand on top of the hand holding my wrist.

"You know how little kids try to coax you along to get what they want?" Shūya said. "Well, maybe I should have done that to get their attention. Someone could have said, *I found a dead cat in a field*. Really?...well, actually I'm the one who killed it. *No!*...But it's true! Sometimes I kill cats and dogs. *No!...you really do?* But I don't just kill them. *What do you mean?* I use the Execution Machine I invented. *You're kidding! That's fantastic!*...Open it. There's a surprise inside...Mizuki, do you think I'm a murderer? Mizuki? What am I supposed to do now...?"

Shūya was crying, and I had no idea what to tell him. So I

just held him in my arms. I'm not sure why, but the alarm on the lie detector went off again.

It was nearly dawn when I got home the next day.

Werther was really happy when he realized that the bullying had stopped. Shūya was smiling again in class, and he got the top scores of the entire grade on the final exams. Everybody assumed that Yūsuke would be elected class representative, but then some kids started saying how they might even vote for Shūya. Werther seemed elated. I even saw him winking at Shūya once in the hallway as he was being complimented by one of the English teachers. It made me want to puke.

But Werther still had a big problem: Naoki. If he didn't start coming to school again soon, he wouldn't be able to graduate and go on to high school and college.

I'm not really sure how you feel about this, but I've been thinking about what it takes to admit you can't do something when you really can't do it. I know you don't like kids to give up when they haven't even tried—I know that's wrong—but I think you also have to be really brave to admit you can't do something when you really just can't. I guess what I'm saying is that I wish Werther had been brave enough to admit that he couldn't get Naoki to come to school.

Or maybe if he'd just talked to one of the other teachers about it. Maybe they could have suggested that he go to some other school or something—

Because the reason he couldn't come to school was right here in this class.

*　*　*

After school on the day before first quarter ended, Werther and I went to pay our usual visit to Naoki's house. It was about six o'clock, but the sun was still high in the sky and I was really sweaty as we stood outside the door.

I'd brought along a letter I'd written to Naoki that day, because I didn't think it was fair to tell Shūya the results of the test on the milk carton and not tell Naoki. Of course I didn't think I could just tell him what I knew and get him to come back to school. I didn't really care whether he came or not. I just wanted to give him one less thing—a really big thing—to worry about.

Naoki's mother had barely opened the door when Werther handed her the class notes in an envelope and the card we'd all signed, which he'd wrapped up like a present. I was amazed he hadn't brought the card before this—and I wished he had forgotten about it altogether.

When her arm came out of the crack in the door, I could see she was wearing a heavy, long-sleeved shirt. Maybe she had the air conditioner on, but it still seemed a little weird for such a hot day. I didn't really get a good look at her face. But I did try to hand her my letter before she shut the door—but just then Werther wedged his foot in the crack and started to yell.

"Naoki! If you're in there, listen to me! You're not the only one who had a hard time this term! Some of your classmates have been bullying Shūya! It's been pretty bad! But I've managed to convince them that they're wrong. It wasn't easy, but

I did! They got it! So how about it, Naoki? I know you're hurting, but I think I can help! Why don't you give it a try! I think we can face your problems together. And I know I can help you solve them! I want you to trust me! I want you to come to school tomorrow, come to our closing ceremony. We'll be waiting for you!"

As I stood there listening to him, I got really, really mad. He'd been so wrong—about everything. He'd said they weren't bullying Shūya, that they were really jealous of him, but now that it's stopped, he calls it bullying. When I looked up at Naoki's window, I thought I saw the curtains move a little.

Werther was so worked up by this point that he looked pretty crazy. His eyes were all buggy and out of focus as he bowed to Naoki's mother and shut the door. You could see some of the neighbors looking at us from their windows, but Werther just smiled at them and turned to me.

"Mizuho," he said, "I want to thank you for coming with me all this time." He was talking to me, but his voice was a lot louder than it needed to be—loud enough for everybody on the street to hear him. It was almost like he'd been putting on a show from the start, and I'd been his audience from the first act right through to the final curtain. I'd been brought along as the witness, so I could testify to the fact that he'd made all these "house calls," that he'd been a totally devoted teacher. I felt the letter I'd brought, still in the pocket of my skirt, and I crumpled it into a ball.

That night, Naoki killed his mother.

* * *

They cut short the closing ceremony for the first quarter and the PTA ran a special meeting for us that afternoon.

"Last night, one of your classmates was involved in a serious incident. We still don't know all the details, but we want you to know that you're not in any danger." That was all the principal told us—but everyone knew anyway. We'd been talking about it in class and we knew Naoki had done something terrible, but we wanted to know more. There was a strange excitement in the room. We went back to homeroom after the closing ceremony, but Werther said nothing about it. I could tell he wanted to talk to us, so the school must have put on some kind of gag order. Then homeroom ended and everybody was sent home—except me. I was told to stay after. I wasn't surprised, since I'd been at his house just a few hours before it happened. Before he left, Shūya gave me a good luck charm.

I waited for a few minutes and then Werther came back in the room.

"You have nothing to worry about, Mizuho," he said, putting his hands on my shoulders and looking me in the eye. "No matter what they ask, just tell the truth." I looked back at him, holding really still.

"Can I ask you something?" I said at last. He nodded. "But before I do, would you put this on?" He looked skeptical but I told him that it was a good luck charm—that all the kids were wearing them. Then I handed him the lie detector watch that Shūya had slipped me before he left and watched as he strapped it on. "So, were you going to Naoki's house every week because you were really concerned about him?

Or were you just going because it made you feel good about yourself?"

"What are you talking about? That's ridiculous, Mizuho! You were there—you know perfectly well! I was doing it for Naoki!"

Beep, beep, beep, beep...Werther looked down at the flashing face of the watch as the awful sound filled the room.

"What is this thing?" he snarled.

"Don't worry," I told him. "It's just the Last Judgment."

I followed Werther to the school office. The principal was waiting for us, along with the lead teacher for our grade and two police officers. Werther and I sat side by side, and they asked us to tell them everything we could about Naoki— though they still hadn't told us anything more about what had happened. I just told them my story, as Werther had suggested.

"I've been going every Friday with Yoshiteru-sensei to deliver copies of our class notes to Naoki's house. His mother always comes out to meet us, but we haven't seen Naoki once in all the time we've been going. At first, she seemed pretty happy to see us, but lately I've been getting the feeling we're bothering her. Even when it's hot, she's always wearing long sleeves, and sometimes I can tell she has bruises on her face under her makeup. I thought she might be getting them from Naoki—maybe because she tried to get him to go to school every time we showed up at the house.

"She never said anything, but I could tell that our visits themselves were beginning to stress Naoki. He isn't the kind of kid to get angry or hurt anybody, but I suppose he felt backed into a corner when he heard us coming, and he had nowhere else to let off steam. His mother had spoiled him pretty bad, and I guess he tried to hurt her when he couldn't figure out what else to do. I suppose you'd say that he's a little weak. But I think all his other teachers realized that. The only one who didn't was Yoshiteru-sensei—who was convinced he could solve Naoki's problems all by himself. But the more we went, the more Naoki felt trapped and the more he lashed out at his mother. That's why I told Yoshiteru-sensei I thought we should take a break from the visits, but he didn't care what I thought. Instead, he made everything worse the other day when he started yelling up at Naoki's window, so loud that everybody in the neighborhood could hear. It was like he wanted to turn Naoki into a freak or something. I think Naoki thought of his house as a kind of sanctuary, since he couldn't face school. But Yoshiteru-sensei wanted to smoke him out of that one safe place.

"It was almost like Yoshiteru-sensei was hunting him. But he isn't ever thinking about what's best for us anyway. We're just a mirror he uses to stare at his own reflection. None of this would have happened if he wasn't so self-absorbed."

I know it's hard to believe, but all of this has happened in one term—in the four months since you left us. It's summer vacation now, and I'm wondering whether Werther will be coming back for the start of the new term. If he is shameless enough to show up, then I've got some things to figure out.

Since last summer, I've been collecting all kinds of chemicals. If things get too awful, I'm planning to use them as my way out. But I've started thinking that I should test them on someone else first to see if they work. What I really want is some potassium cyanide, and now might be the best time to get it since the teachers are all much more worried about the scandal and their reputations than about the keys to their storage lockers. I bet if I ask Tadao-sensei for his, he'd give it to me, no questions asked.

It should be easy to slip something to Werther if he comes back in the fall. He's the only one who drinks the milk, and I guess I wouldn't care anyway if somebody else got some....

But I suppose you may be wondering why I hate Werther so much. It's because I've been in love with Naoki ever since the first grade. He's my first and only love. I guess it started when that idiot Ayako began calling me Mizuho. She was jealous because she's so dumb and I always knew all the answers—so she made up that stupid nickname and the others joined in. After that I was Mizuho to everybody—except to Naoki, who kept on calling me Mizuki. I'm not even sure why he refused to go along with Ayako—maybe he was just used to Mizuki—but it was enough to convince me that he was my only friend in the world.

One of Naoki's sisters told me that when she asked him why he had killed their mother, he said it was because he wanted the police to arrest him.

Moriguchi-sensei, do you mind if I ask you one last question?

What do you think of your revenge now?

CHAPTER THREE

The Benevolent One

It was early morning on July 20, a few days before I was due to go home for summer vacation during my second year of college, when I suddenly had a call from my father.

He had two pieces of news: one, that my mother had been murdered; and two, that the murderer was my little brother, Naoki.

That made things a little complicated. If your mother is murdered, as a relative of the victim you should hate the murderer; but if the murderer is your brother, then you have to face the criticism that goes along with being a relative of a criminal while worrying about the chances for your brother's rehabilitation and apologizing to the victims—of which you happen to be one!

How do you do all this at once?

One thing's for sure: The press and the hangers-on aren't

going to leave you alone just because it's a private family matter. In no time at all our house was surrounded, and the looks in people's eyes weren't sympathetic, or even particularly mean—just blatantly curious.

Murders aren't as rare in Japan as they used to be. In fact, they're so common that most people just yawn when they hear about one on the TV news. But they can still stir up interest when they offer a look inside the workings of a dysfunctional family—let you see how badly things can go wrong.

Dysfunctional love, dysfunctional discipline, dysfunctional education, dysfunctional human relations. At first, everybody wonders how something like that could happen to such a nice family; but when you poke around a bit the dysfunction comes out, and then you see that it was bound to happen, that it was only a matter of time.

I imagine there are people who see this kind of thing on TV and worry about their own family. But I never really did. It always seemed like it could never happen to us. The Shitamuras were normal—the most "average" family you could imagine. But it did happen: We had our own murder right in the family. So, what made us dysfunctional?

The last time I was home was at New Year's.

On January 1, my mother and father and Naoki and I went to the neighborhood shrine for the ceremonial first visit of the year. Then we came home and sat around eating the traditional food Mother had made while we watched TV. I told my mother about friends I'd made in Tennis Club while we worked in the kitchen, and Naoki talked about this comedian who had come to perform at the school festival.

The next day our older sister came to visit with her new husband, and we all went to the mall to check out the New Year's sales. Naoki's grades had gone up a lot during the second term, so Mom and Dad bought him the laptop he'd been wanting, and I managed to guilt-trip them into getting me a new purse.

It was the same as every other New Year: an average celebration for an average family. I've been over everything we did and said a hundred times and I can't think of anything that might have been a clue to what was coming.

What could have happened in the six months since then that made everything go so wrong?

Mother's body had a single stab wound to the belly and a contusion on the back of the head. They said that she was stabbed with a kitchen knife and then thrown down the stairs. They say.... It all seemed so unreal, and even after I saw her in the morgue, I couldn't really believe she was dead—or that Naoki was the one who had done that to her.

Why did this happen? If I can't figure that out, I won't be able to accept my mother's death. If I can't figure it out, I won't be able to accept my brother's guilt. If I can't figure it out, my father and sister and I won't be able to go on as a family.

I began to learn about my family's dysfunction two days after my mother's death—and it was the police who first started to explain. It seems that Naoki had never been to school after the start of eighth grade. Actually, it's not that rare now for kids to refuse to go to school or even leave the house, but the truly disturbing thing about Naoki's behavior is that my mother was the only one who knew about it. It might be understandable that I didn't know what was going on, since I was living far away, or even that my sister didn't know—she's pregnant and lives in another town—but it's incredible my father knew nothing when he was right there with them in the same house. I understand he had a long commute and worked late most nights, but how could you miss the fact that your son wasn't going to school—for four whole months?

When the police asked him about it, he said he supposed it had something to do with an incident that had occurred during the third term of the previous year. My father is usually pretty quiet, but after all this he seemed like a different person. During the police interview, he rattled on and on in answer to their questions. I won't repeat everything he said, but here's a quick summary.

The daughter of Naoki's homeroom teacher fell in the school pool and drowned. Naoki happened to be there when it happened, but he wasn't able to save her. The teacher felt that Naoki was somehow responsible for her daughter's death, that upset Naoki terribly, and though the teacher resigned, Naoki was unable to bring himself to go to school after that.

Now, I have no doubt that a child as emotionally fragile as Naoki would have trouble coping with something like this. I even believe he might have shut himself away from the world as a result. But I'm not sure I see how this would end with the murder of my mother.

Once he'd stopped going to school or leaving the house,

what did he do all day at home? How did he interact with my mother? Now that she's gone, he's the only one who knows. But I'm not allowed to see him yet. So how was I supposed to find out?

But then I remembered what my mother had said when she bought me a diary as I was first setting off to live alone in Tokyo. "Whenever you're worried or sad about something, I want you to know you can talk to me. But when you can't or don't want to, you should try writing in here. Just imagine you're talking to the person you trust most in the whole world. It's amazing how much the human brain is able to remember, how much you hold onto in life, but when you write something down, you can forget about it—you no longer have to hold it inside. Remember the good things; write the bad ones down in here and forget about them."

Apparently her favorite teacher in middle school had given her a diary and told her pretty much the same thing— as a way of comforting a student who had lost both her parents one right after the other.

So I searched the house and found my mother's diary.

March 13

Yūko Moriguchi, Naoki's homeroom teacher, came to visit yesterday.

I disliked the woman the first time I met her. I even wrote to the principal to say I disapproved of having a single mother in charge of a class of impressionable adolescents— for all the good it did me. A mother's opinion doesn't count for much at a public school. But I was right about her, and the proof came in January of this year when Naoki got into a fight with some high school boys and the police took him into protective custody. The homeroom teacher is responsible in that kind of situation. She *should* have gone down to the station to help him. But this Moriguchi was too busy with her own child and sent another teacher instead. If the principal had moved Naoki to a different homeroom at that point, none of this would have happened.

There was an article in the local paper about how Moriguchi's daughter had drowned in the school swimming pool. I'm sorry, of course, that she lost her little girl, but I have to say I found it odd that she was bringing her to the school in the first place. I doubt that would have been tolerated had she been working anywhere else but a school. You might even say that it was the loose regulations for public employees and her spoiled attitude that caused her daughter's death.

But as if that weren't enough, she suddenly showed up here and started asking Naoki all sorts of questions and making all kinds of insinuations. First she asked him about how he had been getting along at school, and even though she must have known most of it, Naoki told her again. How he'd joined the Tennis Club but had to quit because he couldn't stand the coach, how he'd started going to cram school after that, and how he'd got mixed up with those high school boys at the video-game center and had been punished by the school even though he was the victim.

You could tell from the way he told all this that he'd been excited and happy to start middle school but that things had turned out badly. None of it was his fault, but he was still miserable. As I listened to him, I got madder and madder at Moriguchi. Why was she here? Just to stir up all these bad memories for Naoki? But still this wasn't enough for her. She started asking him what he knew about her daughter's death.

Finally I couldn't help myself. "Why are you asking all this?" I practically screamed at her. "This has nothing to do with Naoki!" But almost before I was done, Naoki said something that nearly made me faint.

"It wasn't my fault," he murmured.

Naoki had become friendly with a classmate named Shūya Watanabe at the beginning of the third term. I had read about him in the paper when he won a prize for a theft-prevention purse he had invented, and at the time I was happy that Naoki was making the right kind of friends. But this Shūya turned out to be a horrible boy.

He decided he wanted to try out his invention on someone, see how they reacted to the electric shock he had rigged up in the zipper, and he forced Naoki to pick the victim. Naoki's too kindhearted to have named any of their classmates, so he suggested one or two of the teachers. But the Watanabe boy wasn't interested in any of them, so Naoki finally mentioned Moriguchi's daughter. I'm sure Naoki thought it was a safe suggestion—that Shūya would never do anything like that to a little girl.

But we weren't dealing with a normal boy—this Watanabe is a real bad seed. He jumped at Naoki's suggestion and immediately started working on a plan. Finally, that afternoon, he dragged Naoki along and they waited for the girl at the pool.

It almost makes me faint when I imagine what it must have been like for Naoki. Apparently he was the one who spoke to the girl when she came to feed the dog—Watanabe was counting on Naoki's wonderful way with people to lure her in. Once the little girl had begun to trust them, Watanabe gave her the pouch in the shape of that rabbit character. He put the cord around her neck and told her to open it.

To tell the truth, I'd seen the pouch myself: Naoki and I had come upon them at the mall just as the little girl was begging Moriguchi for it. I suppose she thought she was teaching her daughter a lesson, but if she had just bought the thing for the child that day, she could have avoided the scene at the store and deprived Watanabe of his bait. Heaven knows she could have afforded it on her salary, even as a single mother.

The girl touched the zipper and collapsed—and Naoki was forced to witness her death. I can't imagine how frightened he must have been. But I think it must have been even more frightening to realize that Watanabe had been intending to kill her all along.

As soon as it was over, he told Naoki that he was free to tell anyone he wanted to, and then he turned around and left. But did Naoki run and tell on him? No, he was too loyal a friend. He decided to cover for Watanabe by trying to make it look like an accident—and so he threw the girl's body in the pool. He told Moriguchi that he was so upset that he really didn't remember much more than that.

"Well," she said, in that condescending tone of hers, "since the police have ruled it an accident, I don't intend to stir up trouble." Stir up trouble? For whom? It was all

Watanabe's fault. He planned the whole thing—Naoki was nothing but his unwitting accomplice, as much a victim as anybody. She may have decided not to tell anyone, but I was so mad I was almost ready to go to the police myself and tell them the whole story.

But Naoki did drop the body in the pool. Would that make him an accessory of some sort? He'd been trying to cover up somebody else's crime—which might be a crime, too. Naoki has so much to look forward to. I couldn't let him get mixed up in something like this and end up charged as an accomplice to murder. So, much as I hated to, I had to pretend to be grateful to Moriguchi, but I was staring daggers at her as she left that day—just under my relieved little smile.

I had no intention of telling my husband anything about this, but that afternoon I began to think it might be a good idea to offer Moriguchi some kind of compensation, a solatium payment of sorts. I wanted the whole thing over and done with, and didn't want her coming back with her hand out later on.

But if it was going to involve a substantial sum of money, that meant I'd have to get my husband involved. So when he got home from work I told him the gist of what had happened and had him call Moriguchi. But as it turned out, she refused the money—which leaves me wondering why she came here in the first place.

My husband said we should report the whole thing to the police. Is he out of his mind? I told him Naoki would be charged as an accomplice, but he said it was still the right thing to do—even for Naoki. I suppose that's the best you can expect from a man—a father—in this kind of situation, but by this point I was feeling sorry I'd ever told him anything. As usual, it's up to me to protect Naoki.

From the beginning I've had trouble believing what Naoki said about all this. It seems more likely that poor Naoki just happened to be there and that horrid Watanabe forced him to go along and to say that he'd been in it from the start. Or maybe it was Moriguchi. Maybe she made the whole thing up. Maybe her daughter really did slip and fall into the pool, and she's the real criminal for bringing her to school in the first place. But because she didn't want to face the truth, she latched on to Naoki and Watanabe, who just happened to be there, and forced them to tell this lie. I bet that's closer to the truth.

How could he have been involved? I would have realized something was wrong...and I know he would have told me the truth without Moriguchi having to force it out of him.

That's got to be it. The whole thing was made up by that pathetic woman. Which means that Watanabe is a victim, too.

It's all Moriguchi's fault.

March 22
Today is the last day of the school year.

I could tell Naoki's been depressed since that visit from Moriguchi, but he has been going to school every day, so I've been trying not to worry.

When he got home today he went right to his room. He didn't come down for dinner, and he went straight to bed without saying good night. I suppose he's been exhausted from the tension and it all came out at once.

He's got some time to rest now during vacation, but it makes me sad to think that Moriguchi will still be there when he goes back for the new school year in April.

March 27

From the first day of the break I noticed that Naoki has been acting a little odd—almost as if he'd suddenly become a neat freak—or developed obsessive-compulsive disorder.

The first sign was when he asked me to serve dinner on individual plates rather than in one big bowl for all of us. And that from a boy who had always been happy to eat leftovers off my plate or anyone else's. Then it seemed like there was a new announcement every day: He wanted his laundry done in a separate load, he didn't want anyone getting in the bath after he'd used it.

I've seen things like this on TV and I decided it was just a phase, something to do with puberty, so I've done as he asks. I'm not sure that's the best course, but it's clear for now that he really doesn't want me touching anything he wears or uses.

He's never had to do housework of any kind, but now suddenly he's washing all his own dishes and doing all his laundry. Only his own, of course.... As I'm writing this I realize it must sound as though he's suddenly become a model child, but when I actually see him doing all this cleaning, I can't help feeling terribly worried. He spends a whole hour scrubbing just a few plates and cups. Then he puts the whites and the colors into the washing machine together, adds way too much bleach, and runs the wash cycle over and over again. He acts as though all the germs out there in our environment had suddenly become visible to him.

Yet if that were the extent of it, I suppose I could just accept it as an extreme form of OCD and try to figure out what to do about it. But Naoki's trouble is worse. At the same time he's cleaning everything around him, he's doing just the opposite to himself.

He's getting filthy. He refuses to do anything to clean his body. I keep telling him he's got to take care of himself, but he's stopped combing his hair or brushing his teeth. He used to love taking a bath, but now he won't go anywhere near it. He was walking down the hall today and I jokingly gave him a tiny little shove in the direction of the bathroom door, but he turned around and screamed, "Don't touch me!" in a tone of voice I've never heard from him before. It was really the first time he's ever raised his voice to me at all. I tried telling myself that he's going through a rebellious phase, but it made me terribly sad all the same.

But a few minutes later he came to find me like nothing had happened and started talking about things he remembered from years ago. It was so strange—I don't know how much longer I can take this.

March 31

One of the neighbors came over today with some bean cakes they'd brought back from a trip to Kyoto. Naoki has never been fond of bean sweets, but I decided to take some up to his room anyway to see if he might be interested.

I wasn't surprised when he refused, but then he showed up in the kitchen a little while later and said he'd changed his mind and wanted to try them. I made a pot of tea and we sat down. I have to admit I was nervous.

He took a little nibble and then shoved the whole cake in his mouth and swallowed it in one bite. Then, for some reason, he started to cry.

"I never knew they were so delicious!" he said. "I never knew!"

It was when I saw him crying that I realized all his cleaning and his self-neglect have nothing to do with puberty or a rebellious phase or OCD or anything else. It's all because of what happened with the Moriguchi girl.

"Eat as many as you want," I told him.

He took another cake out of the box and unwrapped it, and this time he ate it slowly, one bite at a time—and I'm pretty sure he was thinking about that little girl the whole time he was chewing the cake, mourning a child who would never enjoy a delicious treat like that again. He is truly a sweet boy.

I suspect it's not just when he's eating bean cakes, either. I think he thinks about her all the time, no matter what he's doing. All that compulsive washing must be his way of trying to wipe away that terrible memory; and at the same time he neglects himself and lives in filth because he feels guilty about being comfortable when she's unable to feel anything at all.

He's still punishing himself for what happened.

At last I feel as though I understand why he's been acting so strangely these past few days—and I'm sorry that I didn't realize sooner what he's been going through. He's been asking for my help all along, and I was too blind to see.

This makes me realize all the more that the real villain here is that awful Moriguchi, with her false accusations and evil mind games. If she has to find a way to escape her own guilt, couldn't she at least pick on someone as warped as she is? It's too awful for words, trying to pass on her sins to a sweet boy like Naoki. It's obvious she quit her job because she couldn't escape her own feelings. She would have had to face the same class of children at the start of next year, so the only solution was to leave. I have half a mind to write the principal and ask him to find an enthusiastic young man to take her place.

Naoki needs to stop worrying. What he needs now is to forget the whole thing. And the best way to forget the painful things in life is to write them down in a diary like this.

Come to think of it, it was my favorite teacher in middle school who taught me that. Why was I so lucky, having such a wonderful teacher, while Naoki ends up with a loser like Moriguchi? That's what she is all right: a loser.

He was just a little unlucky. But his luck's about to turn. I'm sure of it.

April 3

I went to the stationery store today and bought a diary with a lock and key. The lock makes it feel as though you're really closing away all the stuff you spill out on the page.

I took it up to him a few minutes ago and told him I knew he had all kinds of troubles bottled up inside.

"But you don't have to keep it all in there," I told him. "And you don't even have to tell me. Just write it down in here."

He is an adolescent boy, so I was worried he might think a diary was too girly, but he took it without saying anything. Then he started to cry again.

"Thanks, Mom. I'm not much good at writing, but I'll give it a try."

By then I was crying, too, but I'm feeling better, trying not to worry. I'm sure he'll be back on his feet soon. I'm sure I can help him forget about all this unpleasantness.

I'm sure.

April 8

I usually write down bad things I'm trying to forget here in my diary, but today I feel as though I have to write about something that makes me very happy.

Mariko came by to tell me she's pregnant! She's only in her third month and she's not showing yet, but you could tell by the look on her face—confident and happy and ready to be a mother.

She brought along Naoki's favorite, cream puffs, and we were going to have a little celebration, just the three of us, but when I went up to his room to get him he refused to come down. He said he thought he was catching a cold and didn't want to pass it on to his sister.

Mariko seemed a little disappointed, but she said that Naoki was a lot more considerate than her husband, and then she started complaining about the way he had been smoking around her even though he knew it wasn't good for a woman in her condition.

She grumbled on and on, but I wasn't really listening. I was realizing that I'd been misreading Naoki. I'd been so focused on his strange behavior that I'd lost sight of Naoki himself. He wasn't just my sweet boy; he'd grown and matured to the point that he could show real consideration for his sister. It made me truly happy to realize that.

It made me even happier when he leaned out the window as she was leaving and waved to her. "Congratulations, Mariko!" he called.

"Thanks, Naoki," Mariko called, waving back as she started down the street.

As I watched the two of them, all the doubts I'd been having about my skills as a mother vanished. The children had turned out all right.

I was raised in the most wonderful family. My father was strict, my mother the model wife, and they had my brother and me—the perfect family. All our relatives and neighbors made a point of saying how much they admired and envied the four of us. My father let my mother run the household while he worked like a dog day and night to provide for us; and thanks to his efforts we were a little better off than most of the other families around us.

My mother was strict with me, looking after my training and making sure I had the kind of upbringing—manners, etiquette, and all the little details—that would let me hold my head high no matter where I went or whom I married. My brother, on the other hand, was spoiled and coddled and praised. He was taught to be confident and to do exactly as his opinions and preferences dictated. My mother was determined to provide a home life that would let my father focus all his energies on work, so she took it upon herself to solve any problems that arose.

But I suppose it was because we were so fortunate that those tragedies came to us one after the other. While I was in middle school, my father died in an automobile accident and my mother fell ill and followed him soon after. My brother is eight years younger than I am, so he was just a boy when we were taken in by relatives—and because of the difference in our ages, I began to act as a surrogate mother to him from that point. Following my mother's example, I was strict with myself but treated my brother with great care and indulgence. I like to think that's why he was able to get into a top university, find work in a prestigious company, build a fine home for himself, and flourish in life.

That may explain why I feel nothing can go wrong if I follow my mother's example.

Naoki continued to show symptoms of OCD combined with self-neglect—I can't think of any better way to describe his condition—but after I gave him the diary, he seemed to be in a good mood a bit more often.

I have also begun to realize, now that I think back, that my two older girls had phases like this, too. Mariko was in middle school when she suddenly announced that she wanted to quit piano lessons, and Kiyomi was about the same age when she started refusing to wear the clothes I bought for her.

Naoki had the bad luck to be caught up in that nasty mess

right at this sensitive moment in his development, and I think he's still trying to figure out what to do next, what his life will become. I have to keep this in mind and try to stay calm. If I continue to praise every little thing he does and show him unconditional love—just as my mother and I did for my brother—then I'm sure I'll get my sweet Naoki back. Or, rather, I'm sure I'll get my Naoki back, but even more grown-up.

He just needs to rest and recuperate while he's still on spring break.

April 14

A couple of years ago you started hearing a lot about young people who were dropping out of society, the ones called *hikikomori*—"shut-ins"—or NEETs. They say there are more and more of them every year and it's getting to be a major social problem.

But when I hear those words, I wonder whether the real problem isn't the names themselves, the whole idea of giving titles to children who stop going to school or looking for work. I believe we find our sense of stability, our place in life, by participating in society, by coming to belong somewhere and taking on the title of that position—mother, teacher, doctor. Not belonging anywhere, not having a title of some sort, means, in effect, that you're not really a member of society. So it seems to me that most normal people, if they found themselves in that situation—without a position or title—would feel terrible anxiety and do everything they could to secure a place in the world as quickly as they could.

But the moment you start calling those young people by

those names—*hikikomori*, NEET, or whatever—those names *become* their titles, their sense of belonging. They can feel right at home, quite comfortable and reassured, knowing that they're full-fledged dropouts with their own recognized condition and function in society. Why, then, would they see any need to make the effort to go to school or find a job?

Once society accepts these names and positions, there's very little we can do about it—but I still can't understand parents who are comfortable calling their own child a *hikikomori* or a NEET. How can they hold their heads up in public? There's only one explanation: They're determined to blame the child's condition on the school or on society, on anything and everything except the situation in their own home.

But they're fooling themselves. The school or society may have something to do with the problem, but a child's personality first and foremost is molded in the home, and you've got to assume the root cause is there, too, on some level.

A child becomes a *hikikomori* because of something in his home life. If that's the case, then Naoki is *definitely not* a *hikikomori*.

The new term started exactly a week ago, but he still hasn't been to school. The first day he said he felt a little feverish, so I let him stay home and didn't make an issue of it. When I called the school, a young man answered and told me he was the new homeroom teacher. It was gratifying to know that the principal had finally seen things my way, and I went straight to Naoki's room to let him know.

"A young man like that is bound to be more sympathetic," I told him.

But he was "feverish" the next day and the day after that and had no interest in going to school. When I tried to feel his forehead, he brushed my hand away and practically snarled at me, and when I gave him the thermometer, he made up another excuse.

"It's not a fever exactly. More like a headache."

I'm sure he's not really ill. But he's not just playing hooky, either. The prospect of going to school brings up that whole incident for him again, and I think that's what's keeping him at home.

Naoki is weary at heart. He needs rest. Which is why I'm going to take him to the doctor and get a medical excuse. If he just stays home without a diagnosis, the neighbors will start calling him a *hikikomori*.

He may not like the idea, but we need to see the doctor just this once. I'll have to put my foot down about this.

April 21

Today I took Naoki to see a psychologist in the next town.

I knew he would put up a fight. But I didn't want to be one of those parents who loses control of her own child—the type who settles for calling him a *hikikomori*.

"If you won't go with me to see the doctor," I told him, "then I want you to go to school right now. But if you'll go and get them to write you a proper excuse, I'll stop insisting you have to go to school. I know you may not realize it, but psychological problems are considered real illnesses nowadays. Just go and talk to them and we'll see."

He thought about it for a minute.

"They won't need to draw any blood?" he asked. He's been afraid of shots since he was a little boy, and it made me love him all the more to realize that's what he was most worried about. He's still just a child.

"Don't worry, I'll tell them not to give you any shots," I said, and with that he started to get ready to go. It was then that it occurred to me that he hadn't been out of the house since the last day of the previous term.

They gave him a quick physical at the clinic and then he received nearly an hour of counseling. No matter what they asked him, however, he just looked at his lap and said nothing. He seemed unable to explain how he was feeling either physically or psychologically, so I had to step in and tell the doctor what's been happening.

I told him that Naoki had been falsely accused of a crime by last year's homeroom teacher and that he no longer felt comfortable going to school. I also mentioned his problems with compulsive cleanliness and the rest of it.

The doctor told us that Naoki is suffering from "autonomic ataxia." He said I shouldn't try to force him to go to school—that the most important thing now was to avoid causing him stress and to help him relax. I was given strict orders to keep him at home.

On the way back I asked Naoki whether he wanted anything to eat. He said he wouldn't mind a hamburger and mentioned a fast food chain he said he likes. I don't care for those places myself, but I suppose at his age he craves that sort of food from time to time. We went into a restaurant across from the station.

I wrapped a paper napkin around the burger so I wouldn't have to touch it, and as I was eating I realized that Naoki had chosen a fast food restaurant because of his new hygiene concerns. In places like this you don't have to use plates and utensils that other people have used before you, and no one else is going to use your dishes after you're finished with them.

A little girl about four years old and her mother were sitting at the next table. I found myself disapproving of the woman for bringing such a young child to a place like this, but then I saw that the girl was drinking milk and I felt a bit reassured. Or I did until she dropped the carton and it splattered on the floor. Milk got on the leg of Naoki's pants and on his shoes, and he turned white as a ghost and went running for the bathroom. I think he lost his whole lunch; he was terribly pale when he came back to the table.

He's almost certainly mentally unstable, but I'm also concerned he's not physically well, either. I'm going to send the doctor's excuse to school tomorrow and let him rest at home for the time being.

May 4

Naoki spends a good deal of his time cleaning now.

His fingernails have grown embarrassingly long, but he endlessly scrubs every dish. He's forever washing and drying his clothes, though they're always wrinkled and mussed. And every time he uses the bathroom, he scours the toilet, the walls, even the doorknob.

I tell him I can do all this, but he pays no attention, and

if I try to help, he screams at me for touching his dishes or clothes. Of course, there's nothing wrong with what he's doing and I know I should probably just leave him alone. But then again, I'm sure this all has to do with what happened at school, and I feel as though I've got to do something.

I know he should be taking a bath at least once a week, but since he's not going outside he's not sweating or getting dirty, so it hasn't become too unpleasant.

Teatime is my favorite moment in the day, and if Naoki's in a good mood, I bring out a treat—a trick I learned after the neighbors brought those bean sweets. We sit eating together, and sometimes he'll even tell me he's hungry for my special pancakes. He no longer comes along with me when I go shopping, but at least I can enjoy picking out something he likes when I'm in the store.

I'm not really sure what he's doing the rest of the time— working on his computer, playing video games, sleeping— but he's always up in his room and he makes very little noise.

Perhaps he's just taking a little break from life.

May 23

Naoki's new homeroom teacher, Yoshiteru Terada, was kind enough to pay us a visit today.

I had spoken with him on the phone several times, but meeting him in person I was extremely impressed with his energy and dedication. Naoki said he did not want to come out of his room, but Terada-sensei listened very carefully to what I had to tell him.

He also brought along copies of the notes from all of

Naoki's classes. I was particularly grateful to him for this since I've been worried about Naoki's studies. He may need time to rest at home, but I don't want him to fall behind in school. This Terada seems like an extremely caring and concerned teacher.

The one thing that bothered me, however, was the fact that he brought Mizuki Kitahara along with him. He may have been thinking that having a classmate here would help Naoki relax, but I wish he'd chosen someone who didn't live right here in the neighborhood.

I've been in touch with the school about Naoki's condition, but I don't know what Terada-sensei has told his class. If Mizuki goes home and tells her parents that Naoki has become a *hikikomori* and they tell their friends, then the whole town will know in no time. But I will call the school tomorrow to thank Terada, and I may also ask whether he could get the class to write something to Naoki to perk up his spirits.

I went up afterward to give Naoki the notes they had brought, but when I opened the door to his room he threw a dictionary at me and yelled something horrible—about being a foolish old hag and blabbing to everybody. I thought my heart was going to stop. I had never seen him act like that or use such awful language. I'm not even sure why he was so upset. Later on I made him a hamburger, his favorite, but he didn't come down to dinner.

But I think Terada-sensei might be able to help Naoki, and that gives me the courage to go on.

June 12

Naoki's obsessive behavior continues, but he may have grown tired of washing dishes. He asked me today to start serving his meals on paper plates. He also wants to drink out of paper cups and use disposable chopsticks. It sounds terribly wasteful, but if that's what it takes to keep him calm, I'll go and get everything tomorrow.

He hasn't taken a bath in more than three weeks, and he wears the same clothes and underwear day after day. His hair is greasy and his body has started to give off a sour smell. Finally, I couldn't stand it any longer and I brought a damp towel to wipe his face even though I knew he'd be upset. But he shoved me away and I fell and hit my head on the banister.

He no longer comes down for his afternoon snack.

But he's still cleaning the toilet.

He seemed to be calming down for a while, but now he's terribly agitated. How did he get like this? ... I'm afraid it's these visits from his teacher and Mizuki. They come every Friday, and I've begun to notice that Naoki stays locked in his room for longer and longer periods around their visits. He knows I've said he can stay at home for the time being, but I suspect they're causing him to wonder whether he can trust me on this, or whether I'm secretly trying to get him to go back to school.

As for Terada-sensei, his energy and enthusiasm had filled me with hope, but as time goes by and he comes back again and again, I've realized he isn't accomplishing anything. He brings the notes, but he seems to have no idea what to do beyond that, no plan or strategy at all. He must be discussing

Naoki's problem with the principal and the head teacher for the grade, but it's a mystery what they're thinking.

I've thought of calling the school to ask for help, but I'm afraid if Naoki got wind of it he might stop coming out of his room altogether, so for the time being I'm going to have nothing to do with the school.

July 3

We live in the same house, but it's been days since I last saw Naoki. He no longer comes out of his room at all.

When I take food up to him—on paper plates—he asks me to leave it outside his door and waits until I'm gone to get it. He hasn't had a bath in over a month, and there's no sign that he ever changes his clothes.

He does have to come out to use the bathroom, of course, but he seems to pick times when I'm out or busy with something. When I come home, I often find the toilet freshly scrubbed but a sour smell lingering in the air. Not a bathroom smell—more like the stench of rotting food.

Naoki seems to see himself as a warrior of some sort—his armor is the filthiness of his body, and his room is his besieged castle.

I had thought he would get over all this if I just watched and waited. But he seems to be cutting himself off more and more each day. I suppose I'm going to have to confront his fears and anxieties myself.

July 11

Dressed in his armor of filth, Naoki lies sound asleep in his frighteningly neat room. If all goes well, he'll stay that way until sometime this evening.

I'm not proud of having slipped a sleeping pill in his lunch, but I couldn't think of any other way to get him cleaned up—get this filthy armor off of him. I'm convinced that his filth—itself a product of his feelings of guilt—is what keeps him locked away from the world.

The curtains were closed and his room was dark, so I had to get close to the bed—despite the smell—to see his face. His skin had been beautiful, but there were sore-looking pimples coming up in the grease and grime, and his hair was covered in crusty dandruff. Yet I still couldn't resist the urge and rubbed my hand gently along his cheek.

Then I brought the scissors in my other hand close to the shaggy hair above his ear. The scissors—the same ones I'd used when I was sewing a little bag for his school supplies in first grade—made a loud clack as I took the first snip of oily hair, and I was worried he would wake up, but somehow I managed to give him a haircut of sorts.

I hadn't really been intending to give him a haircut at all. I just wanted to make it look so bad that he would want to go to the barber. I just wanted to put a chink in his armor, so to speak.

The clippings fell all over the bed, but it occurred to me that they might make him itchy and convince him to take a bath, so I did what I could and left him sleeping there.

A cry like the howl of a beast came from upstairs just as I was starting to make dinner. It was so inhuman that it took me a moment to realize it was Naoki. When I did, I ran up the stairs and gingerly opened the door to his room—only to have his laptop come flying out at me. The room, which had been neat a few hours earlier, was now a complete shambles, and the creature that had been my son was making bloodcurdling sounds and throwing everything he could reach against the walls.

"Naoki, stop!" I screamed, so loudly I surprised myself. And he did. He froze, and then turned slowly to look at me.

"Get out," he said, his voice completely flat.

I realized then that he had gone mad. And I suppose I should have taken my life in my hands and simply embraced him, held on no matter what he did. But for the first time in my life I was terrified of my own child, and I found I couldn't stand to be in the same room with him. I ran from there as fast as I could.

I realized I couldn't handle this alone any longer, and decided to talk to my husband, tell him what's been going on. But then I got a text message on my phone—which I almost never use—telling me that he had to work late and might not be coming home at all tonight.

There's nothing I can do but write all this down here in my diary.

Naoki's room is right above me, and it's quiet again, so perhaps he's fallen back asleep.

July 12
I must have nodded off in the living room while I was writing, but sometime before dawn I woke to the sound of the shower coming from the bathroom. I thought my husband

must have come home, but I found Naoki's clothes in the dressing room instead.

He decided all on his own to take a bath. It's hard to imagine after seeing the way he was last night, but perhaps sleep had calmed him down and he'd reconsidered.

So my strategy of opening a chink in his armor had worked!

The shower ran for more than an hour, and I found myself worrying that he might be contemplating something radical—suicide, even—so I kept going to the bathroom door to listen. But each time I could hear the sound of the stool on the tiles or the scrubbing of a washcloth, so I went back to the living room to wait. It was his first bath in nearly two months, so of course it was going to take time.

I'm afraid I let out an audible gasp when he finally did come out of the bathroom. He had completely shaved his head.

It was shocking, but I realized it was the most hygienic solution. With his head shaved like that, he looked like a monk who had shed all of his worries. His fingernails had also been trimmed, and he had changed into some new clothes I had bought him.

But to be honest, the Naoki standing before me wasn't a very reassuring sight. His face was completely expressionless—as though, along with the dirt, he had washed away every trace of human feeling.

I didn't know what to say to him, but he spoke up first.

"I'm sorry about all this," he said, his voice as flat as his expression. "I'm going to the store for a minute."

Not only had he taken a bath, he was ready to leave the house? I blurted out that I would go with him, but he said he wanted to go alone. Of course, my first instinct was to follow him, but I worried he might spot me and that might undo everything I'd worked for since last night, so I forced myself to sit down and wait for him to come back.

As I watched him head down the street, I realized for the first time the seasons had changed—spring is long over and summer is here.

July 17
What I'm going to write about here—Naoki's trip to the store—happened just a half hour or so after the events in my last entry. But several days have passed and I've been too upset to get to my diary.

After he left, it occurred to me he'd want breakfast when he got back, so I went to the kitchen and started making scrambled eggs with bacon, one of his favorites. Then my cell phone started ringing—as I said before, it almost never does.

I had a bad feeling about the call, and I was right. It was the manager of the convenience store down the street calling to say that he was holding Naoki and I should come right away.

I'd been worried he might do something reckless—shoplifting, for example—so I'd given him plenty of money before he left, but I knew he was still upset and thought he might have taken something on impulse.

But it was nothing as simple as shoplifting. According to the manager, Naoki had come into the store and wandered around the aisles for a while. The manager had seen him putting his hand in his pocket and had assumed he might be stealing, but then he took his hand out of his pocket and walked back through the store, rubbing his palms on the drinks and food on the shelves. It was odd behavior, to be sure, but not in itself cause for detaining a child—except that Naoki had been smearing the store's wares with the blood dripping from his hand. His right hand was wrapped in a bandage—which the manager said Naoki had taken from the shelf and applied by himself after they had stopped him. They had found a razor blade—stolen from our bathroom—in his pocket.

The manager said nothing like this had ever happened before and he wasn't sure what to do, so he'd decided to call the first number in the contact list on Naoki's phone—mine. Naoki refused to say anything to the manager or anyone else in the store, but since no actual crime had been committed, they decided not to call the police, and I was able to make the whole thing go away by buying everything in the store that he had touched.

He was quiet on the way home, too. Since I'd been making breakfast, I went back to the kitchen. Naoki followed and sat down at the table. Perhaps he didn't want to go back to his room now that it was in shambles. I was carrying bags filled with all the bloody things I'd bought. Setting them on the table, I sat down across from him.

Then I asked him why he'd done such a terrible thing. I didn't really expect an answer, but I couldn't keep myself from asking. But he did have an answer.

"I wanted to get arrested," he said, his voice totally empty of emotion.

"Arrested? Why? What do you mean? Are you still thinking about what happened with Moriguchi-sensei's daughter? You didn't do anything wrong! You've got to stop worrying about this."

He didn't answer, but I realized this was the first time we'd actually even mentioned the whole thing. I wanted to be as positive and cheerful as possible, realizing that this might be his one chance to turn the corner and get back on track. "I'm starving!" I said. "And you know what, I've never had a convenience store rice ball. I might as well try one, since we've got so many."

I took a rice ball out of one of the bags. The label identified the flavor as tuna and mayonnaise, but the wrapper was covered in brown streaks of Naoki's blood.

"You probably shouldn't eat that. You might catch AIDS." So saying, Naoki took it from me, peeled off the wrapping, and began to eat it himself. I had no idea why he'd done that—or why he'd mentioned AIDS—and told him so.

"Moriguchi-sensei gave me milk infected with the AIDS virus." Somehow, his tone and expression remained absolutely neutral even as he was telling me this horrible news. As the words ran around in my head, I could feel goose bumps form all over my body.

"That can't be true," I said.

"But it is. She told us what she'd done on the last day of school. That crusading teacher, Sakuranomi-sensei, was actually her daughter's father. You remember him—you said you liked his books. They said he was dying of cancer, but it was actually AIDS, and it was his blood that Moriguchi-sensei put in our milk, Shūya's and mine."

Throughout this gruesome confession, his expression had been flat and empty, but as he finished a look that seemed almost cheerful crept over his face. Unable to sit still any longer, I hopped up, went to the sink—and vomited again and again.

Moriguchi had to be nothing less than a monster to have infected my dear sweet Naoki with HIV, the AIDS virus. And he'd had to bear this awful secret all by himself, without telling anyone—not even me. His obsessive behavior and his self-neglect, his tears when he ate the bean sweets...it all made sense now. I found myself overwhelmed with gratitude that he was still alive.

"I want you to go to the hospital with me," I told him. "I'll explain everything to them."

I wanted them to do something immediately, perhaps even drain all Naoki's old blood and replace it. I was getting more and more worked up, but Naoki was utterly calm. Perhaps because he wasn't finished. The next words out of his mouth were an even worse nightmare and sent me to even lower depths of the hell I'd already fallen into. I don't think I can summarize, so I'll try to write it down just as it was.

"I don't need a hospital," he said. "We should go to the police."

"The police? Of course, we need to have them arrest Moriguchi."

"Not her. I want them to arrest me."

"What do you mean? Why should they arrest you?"

"Because I'm a murderer," he said.

"Don't be ridiculous! You didn't kill anyone. I'm not even sure I believe what you said about dropping the body in the pool, but even if you did, that's not murder."

"Moriguchi-sensei said she was only unconscious, that she died because I dropped her in the water."

"That's absurd! But even if she did, you didn't know, so it's still an accident."

"No," he said. "You're wrong." A smile spread over his face. "She opened her eyes while I was standing there holding her. And then I dropped her in and let her drown."

I can't write anything more today.

July 19

That idiot Terada was just here again, and he behaved even more terribly than usual. He stood outside our door and yelled about Naoki staying home from school in a voice so loud the whole neighborhood must have heard. And he even had the nerve to bring along a big card that Naoki's classmates had made for him—with a perfectly ghastly message picked out in bright red marker.

Don't worry! Imagine happiness! Everyone wins! Maybe you too? Unless you don't? Remember everything! Don't ever forget! Everyone knows! Really we do! Everyone knows! Remember!

They must have thought they'd created a marvelous code—one that Terada was apparently too stupid to figure out—but I saw it almost immediately. The first letters spelled out "Die! Murderer!" Naoki is a murderer...a murderer who has to put up with this terrible abuse from stupid children who have nothing better to do to amuse themselves.

But they did help me make up my mind.

Before this, I had decided that Naoki had dropped Moriguchi's daughter in the pool after Watanabe killed her—and nothing more. I'd been convinced that Moriguchi had made up even that part. The truth was considerably more horrible. He had dropped her in the pool after she'd regained consciousness. In other words, the murder had been intentional.

When Moriguchi came and questioned Naoki until he confessed, I had been convinced he was lying and that it was Moriguchi herself who had forced the lie out of him. That's why I was sure he was innocent. But now I see that he was lying even then, quite intentionally.

I didn't want to hear the terrible truth he had finally told me, but I no longer thought he was lying. I am Naoki's mother, and a mother can tell when her own son is telling the truth.

"But I'm sure it was because you were frightened. You threw her in the pool after she opened her eyes because you were afraid." I repeated this over and over to Naoki. I knew how foolish I sounded, like a mother blinded by love for her child, but once I'd been forced to admit that Naoki had committed murder, I was looking for one last shred of hope—that he'd done this horrible thing because he was terrified.

But he refused me even this.

"If that's what you want to believe," he said. He had no intention even now of telling me why he had killed that little girl. Yet he seemed relieved, as though he had done just that—had gotten everything off his chest—and when I asked him again and again whether he'd been afraid, he just said we should "go tell the police," as though he was humoring a crazy woman.

When he washed away the filth he was using as a shield, I think he must have also washed away the sweetness he'd had since he was a baby. He is no longer the Naoki I love. He has lost all trace of human kindness and become a murderer and a defiant son—and there is just one thing a mother must do in that case.

Yoshihiko, I'm grateful to you for all these years we've spent together.

Mariko, I'm sorry I never got the chance to see your baby. Take good care of my grandchild.

Kiyomi, stay strong and follow your dreams.

I'm going to join my dear mother and father and take Naoki with me.

*   *   *

I thought that if I was willing to root around in the darkness, I might discover the truth, and that might help me find a tiny crack of light, the beginning of a way out. But now that I've finished reading my mother's diary I don't see anything like that—I can't even see my own way forward.

My mother had tried to kill my brother before she took her own life. When I first heard that he'd become a *hikikomori*, that's what I'd assumed. Mother had been so obsessed with her ideal family life. That had been her one source of happiness. So much so that killing Naoki to avoid having to face the destruction of that ideal might have made sense to her.

But the truth wasn't quite so simple. She had actually been willing to let Naoki stay home, having convinced herself that he needed a kind of "time out" from life. She was a woman who couldn't sit still—always fussing over this or that—so it must have taken a great deal of willpower just to watch and wait while my brother sat up in his room.

I don't think it was the sleeping pills and the haircut that sent my brother over the edge. He was already at the breaking point, and it was just a matter of time before he had to confess what he'd done.

Still, things might have ended differently. If they'd been able to hold out just a few more weeks, I'd have come home from school. Now that I've read the diary, I'm not sure what I'd have done, how I could have helped with Naoki, but at least there would have been two of us in the house. We might have figured out something.

Two in the house.... I still wonder how my father could have missed the whole thing. Or whether he actually knew what was going on and just pretended he didn't.

I know Mother would have been furious with me for thinking this, but I suspect that Father was pretending to be mildly depressed as a way to avoid dealing with Naoki's troubles—or maybe he really was depressed because of

Naoki's troubles. But then Naoki's trouble—his fundamental weakness—was probably something he got from Father in the first place....

I suppose our real family could never have lived up to the ideal—and it was always only an ideal—that Mother had in her head. But looking back on it now, I realize that we really were a normal, happy family...until all of this happened.

The shock caused my sister to have a miscarriage, and she's still hospitalized. The reporters and photographers have been poking around—even following her to the clinic—and I suppose it's just a matter of time before they connect the dots and figure out that Naoki was involved in the incident at school. Probably not much longer now.

They've tried to question Naoki, but he says nothing.

I'll probably have to give Mother's diary to the authorities, and when they realize that she was intending to kill Naoki—and that he'd already been treated by a psychologist—he'll probably be found innocent.

Which is what we all want. For Mother's sake, for Mariko's and mine, and even for Father's, I want them to find Naoki innocent.

But that can only happen once they find out what he was really thinking.

CHAPTER FOUR

The Seeker

A white wall in front of me. Another in back. To the right
and left, above and below, white walls.

How long have I been here? Alone in this small, white
room. No matter which way I turn, the same scene plays endlessly on the wall.

How many times have I seen it? It seems to be starting
again....

The snot-nosed middle school kid stumbles along—the first day.
I'm walking along, back hunched against the cold wind,
when the tennis team, in shorts and t-shirts, runs past me.
Then some kids sprinting to the station to get to cram school.
I haven't done anything wrong—I'm just headed home—
but somehow I feel guilty and hunch my back even more,

look down to avoid meeting their eyes, pick up my pace. Even though there's nothing to do when I get home....

I just didn't connect. Ever since starting middle school, I just didn't connect. With what? With other people—with the teachers especially. The tennis coach, the cram school staff, my homeroom teacher—they were all hard on me, harder than they were on anybody else. And the kids noticed, and they're all making fun of me now, too.

I eat lunch with the two biggest dorks in the class—a train fanatic and a kid who spends all his time playing porno video games. I don't have much choice: After I got in trouble in class the first time, they were the only ones who would even talk to me. But it doesn't mean we're friends, or that they treat me well. They're not really interested in anything except trains and porn. They talk to me, so I answer. That's all. I suppose it's better than being alone. But I don't like to be seen with them, especially by the girls in our class.

I don't want to go to school. But I can't really tell my mom why. She'd be too disappointed. The truth is, everything about me must disappoint her. She wants me to be the best at everything—like her brother, Uncle Kōji.

So she tells all her relatives and the neighbors that I'm a really "nice" boy. Nice? What does that even mean? I can't remember ever having done *anything* that could be called nice—I've never once done volunteer work or anything like that. She's got nothing to brag about when it comes to me, so she says I'm "nice." But if that's the best she can do, she shouldn't bother. I don't want to be the worst, but I don't have a complex about not being exceptional.

I grew up thinking I was really smart and really good at sports—because my mother was always telling me I was, from the time I was little. But by third grade I knew that what she was telling me was just her hope, the way she wanted me to be. If I tried really hard, I might end up being a little above average, but I'd never be anywhere near the best at anything.

She kept this up all the way through elementary school. For example, she framed a certificate for the only award I ever received and put it in the living room to show visitors. It wasn't much of an award—third place in a calligraphy contest. I remember I wrote the word *election* in cursive, and the teacher said it looked really "natural."

Once I got to middle school, she didn't even have that kind of stuff to brag about, so she started saying how "nice" I was. But that wasn't enough; then she started writing these letters to the school. I realized what she was doing after midterm exams.

Moriguchi-sensei told us in homeroom who'd gotten the top three total scores. You could tell by looking at these kids that they were all really smart, and I clapped for them along with everybody else. It didn't much bother me that I couldn't get grades like that. I knew I wasn't at that level. Mizuki, who lives in our neighborhood, was the second best, but when I told my mother at dinner that night, she just looked bored. "You don't say?" she said, but I could tell she didn't care.

A few days ago I found a copy of a letter she'd been writing in the wastebasket in the living room. She must have made a mistake and started over.

At this late date, when we've long ago learned the importance of valuing each child for his or her individual talents, I find it deeply disturbing that a teacher should be taking the exclusionary step of announcing the top grades to the other students in the class.

I knew right away that she was writing to complain about Moriguchi, so I took the letter and went to find her in the kitchen.

"You can't send this," I told her. "You'll make it look like I've got some sort of complex because I'm a lousy student."

"Now, Naoki," she said, in her sweetest voice, "that's not it at all. It has nothing to do with you. I just don't like all this attention paid to grades. I'm objecting because that's the only thing she talks about. Is that all that matters? What about being a good *person?* She doesn't seem to care about that. She's not announcing the names of the three nicest children in class, is she? Or the names of the three hardest workers when it comes to cleaning up after school? I just want her to be fair, to balance things out."

I felt like puking. What she was saying sounded reasonable, but if I'd been one of the three with the top grades, she would never have written a letter like this. Bottom line: She was just disappointed in me.

Since then, every time she says how nice I am, it makes me feel more and more miserable. More and more.

A bicycle bell rang behind me and I turned around to see a girl from my class coming up to pass me. She'd been friendly enough until recently—she might have called out as she rode by on her bike. Not now. I pulled out my perpetually silent cell phone and pretended to check my texts, sniffing as if I had a cold. Then I started walking again.

Until somebody hit me pretty hard on the back.

Watanabe. Another kid from the class.

"Hey, Shitamura," he said. "You busy? I've got this awesome video, and I was wondering whether you wanted to watch it with me."

What the...? When we'd switched our desks around in February, we'd ended up next to each other, but we'd hardly ever talked. We hadn't gone to the same elementary school, and we'd never had cleanup duty together after class.

Besides that, he kind of bugged me. I guess we were just too different when it came to schoolwork. He didn't even go to cram school, but his scores were practically perfect in every subject; and over the summer he'd won some sort of prize in a national science contest. But that wasn't even what bothered me most.

Watanabe was usually alone. Before class in the morning or when we had a break, he would be reading some thick book, and after school he would disappear right away. Since I was usually alone, too, I guess you could say we were a lot alike, but what I hated was the fact that being alone obviously didn't bother him.

It wasn't that he didn't have any friends—he avoided people because he didn't want to be with them. Like he couldn't be bothered hanging out with a bunch of idiots. That's what I couldn't take about him. He reminded me of Uncle Kōji.

Still, most of the guys in class looked up to Watanabe, and in a weird way, some of them even tried to suck up to him. But it wasn't because he was smarter than they were—that doesn't get you much respect in middle school—it was because he'd used his smarts to figure out how to almost completely eliminate the blurring the censors put on porn videos and get a clear image. That's what they said, anyway.

I'd heard these rumors and I was as interested as anybody else in getting my hands on the videos, but it wasn't like I was going to ask him out of the blue to lend me one—after all, we'd hardly said a word to each other.

But then *he* came up and started talking to *me*. What the...?

"Why are you asking me?" I said.

I thought he might just be jerking me around. Maybe some of the other guys in class were hiding somewhere nearby to see how I'd react. I looked around, but there was no sign of anyone.

"I've been wanting to talk to you for a while now," he said. "But I could never find the right time. I could tell, though, that you're different from the rest of them. You've got a lot going for you—I'm even a little jealous."

He laughed, sounding almost embarrassed. He had this kind of awkward look on his face. It was the first time I'd seen him smile.

But it still didn't make sense. Jealous? Of me? I might be jealous of him, but the opposite was hard to imagine.

"Why?" I said.

"Everybody thinks I'm an egghead. They think I'm going

all out—I'd do anything to get good grades. It's kind of embarrassing to be seen that way."

"You think so? I don't see you like that."

"Well, everybody else does. I feel like kind of a loser. But you take everything at your own pace. You looked around first term and sized everybody up, and then second term your grades went way up."

"Maybe a little," I said. "But they're still nowhere near as good as yours."

"But you're still on cruise control—you've got a whole other gear. That's pretty cool."

Cool? Me? No one, not another boy or girl, not even my mother, had ever told me I was cool before. I could feel my heart racing, my cheeks getting hot.

It was true that my grades had gone up after summer vacation, when I'd started going to cram school, but they'd long since leveled off. The cram school teacher got on my case and figured out all sorts of ways to make my life miserable—in fact, when I realized that no matter how hard I worked I would never be much better than average, I'd quit cram school last month.

But hearing this now from Watanabe, I began to feel he might be right, that I might actually be coasting. I could probably kick up my game if I wanted to. Maybe I had qualities I'd never recognized myself—ones that only Watanabe could see.

I suddenly wanted to be his friend. More than just about anything.

*   *   *

The next time I saw him we met at his laboratory—a room in an old house by the river. I brought some carrot cookies my mother had made. On a new widescreen TV, zombie doom-bots were swarming through a city at night. As for the porn, he said he'd been interested in figuring out how to get rid of the blurred section on the screen but didn't care about what was behind the blur. In fact, he said it pretty much disgusted him. He let me watch a little, but instead of the normal stuff, it turned out to be all these naked blonde women fighting each other in a regular pro wrestling ring. We turned it off when they started getting really rough.

We decided to watch something else, so we went to the video shop by the station and got an American action-horror movie. Mom doesn't let me watch stuff with guns and lots of violence, so I was pretty into it. The hero was this cool woman who blasted a whole army of zombies with this awesome machine gun, which would be totally fun to do.

In fact, I must have muttered something about "wanting to do that, too," because at some point when I looked over at Watanabe, he was looking back at me.

"Okay," he said. "Is there anybody in particular you want to do it *to?*"

"What do you mean?" I said.

"Wait till it's over," he said, turning back to the movie. I guess I thought he meant "if you were the woman in the movie" or something like that. I went back to watching. The zombies that the woman had just blasted were staggering back to their feet like in some really bad nightmare, and at the end of the whole thing she still hadn't been able to get rid of all of them. I guess there was going to be a sequel.

"What would you do if the whole town was crawling with zombies?" I asked Watanabe, as we ate my mother's cookies. Instead of answering, he stood up, went to a desk, and took something out of a drawer. A black coin purse.

"Is that the Shocking Purse?" I asked him.

"That's right, and I've managed to increase the voltage. I just haven't found anybody to try it out on yet. You want to be the first?" I shook my head and put my hands behind my back. "Just kidding!" he said. "No, I made it to deal with all the people I can't stand. It needs to be tested on one of them."

Then he set the purse down in front of me. It looked like any other change purse with a zipper.

"Does it really work?" I asked.

"If you touch the zipper, you get a pretty good shock— enough to knock you on your ass. Not you—I mean some-body we don't like. How'd you like to see that?"

"You bet I would. But who are you going to use it on?"

"That's the point. I've been so busy inventing this thing and getting good grades, I can't tell people apart—you know, I hate all of them. That's why I was hoping you'd choose."

"Me?" I said, nearly choking. But I was also really excited. We were going to use his invention to get back at someone evil, and I was going to decide who! I felt like I was suddenly in a movie—Watanabe was the mad scientist and I was his assistant.

But who to pick? I racked my brain. Not *my* enemy—*our*

enemy. Which meant it had to be a teacher. One of the more self-satisfied bastards.

"What about Tokura?" I said.

"Not bad...but I don't think I want to mess with him."

Okay, someone else. How about Moriguchi, who was always worrying about her own kid more than her students?

"Moriguchi?" I said aloud.

"Actually, I already tried it on her....I don't think she'd fall for it again."

Strike two. Watanabe sighed and began fooling around with the tools on his desk like he was getting bored. Maybe he was starting to regret he'd asked me to come. If he didn't like my next suggestion, he might even call off the whole plan. Or he might get somebody else to help him—and they'd choose *me*. I could almost hear them talking..."Him? Worthless. A total waste!"

What could be worse? Nothing...except maybe being forced to clean a dirty old pool in winter all by yourself, even though I hadn't even done anything wrong. It wasn't so much the cleaning. I hated having anybody see me being punished like that. So when I heard someone coming, I ducked in the locker room. But it turned out to be—

That's it! What about her?

"What about Moriguchi's little girl?" I said. "She doesn't care about us, just about that brat, so what better way to get to her?"

Watanabe's hand froze over his tools.

"Not *bad!* " he said. "I've never seen her, but I hear she comes to school sometimes."

He was obviously interested. I did a major fist-pump in my head. I had cleared the first hurdle. To seal the deal, to make myself seem really useful, I told him how I'd seen the girl begging Moriguchi for a little pouch at the mall, and how she hadn't bought it for her.

"Awesome! A pouch would give me the room to make it even more powerful. I knew I was right about you, Shita-mura. Thanks to you, this is going to be even better than I thought."

"Then let's go get the pouch. We don't want them selling out."

We got on our bikes and headed for the mall—Happy Town. It was almost Valentine's Day, and the place was really crowded. I wove through all the ladies and the high school girls, making a beeline for the toy corner.

"Here it is! Looks like it's the last one." I smoothed the crushed fur and held out the Snuggly Bunny pouch for Watanabe to see.

"Then it must have been meant to be," Watanabe said. Precisely—if they'd been sold out, the whole plan would have been screwed up. It was fate, us getting the last one.

We put our allowance together and bought the pouch, then we went up to the Domino Burgers on the second floor to hold a strategy session.

"How does the purse work?" I asked him as I bit into my burger.

"It's pretty simple. I can wire a zipper like this to deliver the shock." He arranged French fries on his tray to match the circuits, but I couldn't follow any of it. "You see?" he asked from time to time as the diagram got more complicated.

"I get it," I said, when I thought it sounded right. "It is simple." I didn't want to disappoint him, and as I nodded and pretended to follow along, I almost felt like I was beginning to understand.

But it hardly mattered — I was having more fun than I'd ever had. I'd been to Domino with my sister, but this was my first time with a friend. I remember having seen middle and high school kids here when I was in elementary school and thinking how cool they looked. Now, I was here myself; and to top it off, we weren't just talking about stupid stuff like the kids around us, we were having an important meeting. A secret strategy session.

"But why does she come to the pool?" Watanabe asked, eating one of the French fries from his diagram. That was my cue.

"For the dog. Have you seen the black dog at the house on the other side of the fence?"

"You mean the fuzzy one?"

"That's right. She comes to feed him. I think she hides bread or something under her coat."

"Really? I wonder why she does that? What about the people in the house?"

"Now that you mention it, I haven't seen anyone there in about a week. Maybe they're on a trip. We'd probably need to check on that."

"How?"

"I've got it! What if we throw a baseball over the fence and go into the yard to get it back?" Ideas were popping into my head one after the other. I'd never felt like this before. Watanabe was the chief design officer, but I was in charge of tactics! I wasn't his assistant anymore—we were working together!

I proposed the following plan to him:

1. I would go ahead to scout out the place to avoid any unforeseen interruptions.
2. I'd meet up with him at the pool and we'd hide in the locker room.
3. When the girl came, I'd talk to her first—since Watanabe looks kind of weird when he smiles.
4. Watanabe would hang the pouch around her neck (pretending her mother asked us to buy it for her).
5. Then I'd tell her to look inside.

"Sounds good to me," Watanabe said, sounding satisfied. I burst out laughing, picturing Moriguchi's little girl sitting back on her butt.

"Do you think she'll start bawling?" I asked, still chuckling. Watanabe was giggling, too.

"No, I don't think so."

"Really? I think she will. You want to bet on it? Loser treats for Domino Burgers next time."

"You're on."

We toasted with Coke to seal the deal.

The kid sneaks into the pool feeling really nervous—one week after the first day.

Since this morning—no, really for the past few days—I've been totally pumped. For the first time since I got to middle school, I'm actually happy to be here.

After second period, I whispered to Watanabe, "Everything ready?"

"All set," he whispered back, without looking at me. Even though we were friends now, we hadn't started hanging out at school because we didn't want anyone figuring out what we were up to.

I wasn't really paying attention in class anymore, and in fifth period, during science, when I happened to look up and see Moriguchi, I almost burst out laughing. The whole day seemed to race by.

After school, I went straight to the pool. I took a look around and made sure nobody was there. Fortunately, no one had been given cleanup duty after me.

The dog was sticking its nose through the fence, but it still didn't look like anybody was home. Still, better safe than sorry, so I fished out the baseball I'd found behind the team's shed and threw it into the yard. Then I pretended to be mad that I had to chase it, and I climbed the fence. I walked around the house and pushed the button on the intercom, but there was no answer and no sign of people inside.

Perfect.

I went over the fence again and back to the pool. The dog had been watching me the whole time, but it never once barked. Maybe it was too old—or too stupid.

I texted Watanabe that "Phase One" was completed, and within five minutes he showed up at the pool.

"All systems are go!" I said and gave him the thumbs-up. Then we went into the locker room and hid behind the door. It was never locked. Phase Two under way. The locker room was dark and musty and reminded me of the forts we used to make under a blanket or something when we were kids. Back when I still thought I could do anything. But maybe that had all changed now—maybe I really could do anything, with a friend like Watanabe.

I looked over at him and realized he was doing a final test on the pouch. It looked totally harmless, like a perfectly normal little kid's purse, but I knew better. How cool that it could deliver a real electric shock!

"Why don't you come over to my house next time?" I said. "My mom really wants to meet you. She said she'll bake a cake. I think she's happy I've got a smart friend. She wrote to the principal last term to bitch about Moriguchi always announcing our class rank, but when I told her we were friends she knew right away that you're at the top of our class. Go figure. I don't have anything like your laboratory, but she does bake a pretty good cake. I know, you can come over sometime soon to celebrate this whole plan. I'll have her bake something really special. Which do you like better, whipped cream or chocolate?"

He didn't answer and held his hand up for me to be quiet. Through the crack in the door we could see the girl slipping through the gate.

"It's her," I whispered, and we watched as she made her

way around the pool heading straight for the dog at the fence. Apparently she hadn't seen us.

"Dinner, Muku," she said. Then she squatted down in front of him, pulled some bread out of her jacket, and began tearing off pieces to give to him. He wagged his tail and gobbled down the bread, and she watched him with this big smile on her face. It was all gone in just a few seconds.

"See you soon," she said, wiping the crumbs from her clothes and standing up.

I looked at Watanabe and he nodded. Then we walked slowly over to her. Phase Three under way. I spoke first.

"Hi," I said as we got close to her. "You're Manami, aren't you?" We must have startled her, because she turned around really fast. I kept smiling. "We're in your mother's class. You remember, I saw you the other day at Happy Town."

Everything was going according to plan. Except that she seemed pretty nervous. She was watching us carefully.

"Do you like dogs?" Watanabe asked her. "We do, too. That's why we come here sometimes—to feed the doggie." This line wasn't in the original plan, but the girl got this big smile on her face when she heard it. Watanabe had the pouch behind his back, but as soon as he saw that she'd relaxed, he held it out toward her. Phase Four.

"Snuggly Bunny!" she screamed. Watanabe got this weird smile on *his* face and then he bent down so he could look in her eyes.

"Your mother didn't buy it for you that day, did she?" I asked her. "Did you get one later?" I felt like I was reading a line from our script. She shook her head.

"No?" said Watanabe. "That's why your mother asked us to get it for you. It's a little early, but it's your Valentine present from her." Then he put the cord around her neck.

"From Momma?" she said, looking even happier than before. I didn't think she looked much like Moriguchi until she smiled; then she looked exactly like her.

"That's right. There's chocolate inside. Open it and see." This was the clincher, and it was supposed to be my line, but Watanabe went ahead and said it himself, which made me a little mad. Still, what did it matter? We were getting to the climax. The girl stroked the fur on the pouch for a second and then put her fingers on the zipper.

This was the moment—when she got the shock and fell flat on her ass. Except she didn't.

There was a little popping sound, and she twitched hard and went all floppy, then settled on her back like she was falling in slow motion. After that she just lay there, perfectly still, with her eyes closed.

What just happened? She couldn't be...dead?

As this idea popped into my head, I started to shake and grabbed onto Watanabe almost like a reflex.

"What's wrong? She's not...moving," I said.

Watanabe didn't answer, but when I looked up at him he was smiling. As though everything he'd ever wished had just come true. It was the most natural smile in the world. He looked at me.

"Go ahead, tell everybody all about it," he said.

What? Tell them what? Before I had time to say anything, he brushed me off like a piece of dirt. "See you later," he said, and then he turned around and walked away.

Wait! What did you do? I wanted to scream after him as loud as I could, but nothing came out. He stopped, as though he'd just remembered something, and turned around.

"Oh, I almost forgot. Don't worry about them thinking you had anything to do with this. We've never been friends. I can't stand kids like you anyway—worthless but full of yourself. Compared to a genius like me, you're pretty much a complete failure."

A failure? Wait! Don't leave me here like this! I wanted to run after him, to run away, but my legs were frozen. His words echoed over and over in my head. Everything went black.

It was getting dark. The sound of the evening chime brought me back to my senses. I felt like I'd been standing there in the dark for hours, but it had been only a few minutes since Watanabe had left. His parting words were still racing through my head.

He'd meant to kill her all along. I'd been used. But for what?

Tell everybody all about it. Was that what he'd wanted in the first place? If I went to the police and told them everything that had happened, they'd go and arrest him. Was *that* what he wanted? Did he *want* to be a murderer? Maybe that was it. But if he did get arrested, would they really just let me go? What if he lied to the police? What if he told them he didn't know anything about it? Or that I'd planned the whole thing and had dragged *him* along? That would be it for me.

I looked down and my eyes met the Snuggly Bunny eyes. I was the one who had seen the girl begging Moriguchi for the pouch. I reached down and took it from around her neck, and then I threw it away as far as I could.

Was that enough? Would they suspect me? If I just ran away and didn't tell anybody, would I get off? No, that wouldn't work. If somebody gets electrocuted, they go looking for someone to blame. It wouldn't take long before they'd get Watanabe, and if he turned on me....

But what if I made it look like she fell in the pool? That would work! She just fell in the pool!

I had to act quickly. I picked her up, being careful not to look at her face. She was heavier than I thought she'd be. I staggered across the deck, but when I got to the edge of the pool I nearly fell in myself. The water was dirty and covered with dead leaves. I held out my arms.

No, that wouldn't work. I didn't want to make a big splash and a lot of noise.

I squatted down, taking care not to lose my balance, but as I did the girl's body twitched just a little. Then she slowly opened her eyes. I cried out and nearly dropped her in the water.

She's alive! Alive!

I was so relieved I didn't know whether to laugh or cry.

A *failure*.

As I relaxed from the terror I'd been feeling, Watanabe's last words came back to me again. He had been looking down on me all along, using me. He wanted to be a murderer, and he had exploited me to do it. But the girl was still alive. It was Watanabe's plan that was the *failure*.

You're a failure! You're a failure and you don't even know it! You stupid loser.

I'm not sure which came first: Moriguchi's little girl regaining consciousness and looking up at me...or my letting go and dropping her in the water. But once I'd done it, I left without looking back. My legs weren't shaking anymore.

I'd succeeded where Watanabe had failed.

The kid wakes up with a smile on his face—one day after the incident. My mother was frying eggs and bacon when I went down to the kitchen the next morning. She turned around when she heard me.

"Naoki, something terrible has happened," she said. The newspaper lay on the table. About halfway down the page, a little headline read: "Four-Year-Old Drowns After Sneaking into Pool Area to Feed Dog."

Accidental drowning. It was already in the paper. The article said the whole thing had been ruled an accident. So I'd done it!

"I feel so sorry for Moriguchi-sensei," my mother said. "But I never understood bringing a child to school like that. I wonder what'll happen to your class, especially since you've got final exams in just a few more weeks....But I almost forgot," she said. Then she went over to the dish cupboard and took out a box wrapped in red paper and tied with a gold ribbon. She came over and set it down on the newspaper, covering up the article. "Here you are—chocolate for Valentine's Day."

She smiled and I gave her a big smile back.

Since my sister isn't here anymore, it occurred to me that this was the only chocolate I'd be getting. But then when I got to school I ran into Mizuki and she gave me a little box of chocolate, too—though I guess she had to, since my sister had been nice to her. Not that I was going to turn it down.

"Did you see the newspaper?" she asked me all of a sudden, and I nearly dropped the box. I managed to say something about how terrible it was. When I got to class, that was all anybody was talking about.

Apparently the kids who had stayed late after school were all put to work searching for Moriguchi's little girl. It was Hoshino from our class who had found her, but some other kids had seen the body, too. Everybody was pretty worked up. A few girls were crying, but mostly they seemed kind of excited. At first, they were just trying to figure out what had happened, adding little bits of information, but then it turned into a competition, with everybody bragging about what they'd seen or done.

I was watching all this from the doorway when somebody grabbed my arms from behind and dragged me out in the hall. Watanabe.

"What did you do?" he said, sticking his face right in mine. But somehow I wasn't scared of him. In fact, I suddenly wanted to laugh. I didn't, but I brushed his hand away.

"Don't talk to me," I told him. "We're not friends, remember? And about yesterday? I'm not going to tell anybody. If you want to, go ahead."

I turned around and went back in the class. I sat down, but I didn't join in all the boasting and bragging. I just opened a book, an old mystery novel that Uncle Kōji had given me. I was different now, not the same me I'd been before.

I had succeeded where Watanabe had failed. But unlike him, I wasn't going to tell everybody about it. Moriguchi's little girl died in an accident; and even if they found out it was murder, Watanabe was the one who did it. Anyway, I'd seen how much he'd wanted to do it. If the police showed up at school, he'd probably confess right away.

What an idiot. He had blown the whole thing and he didn't even know it.

Moriguchi took a week off and then showed up at school again. She didn't say anything about what had happened — just apologized in homeroom for having been gone so long. Like she'd had a cold or something.

If I died, my mom would probably turn into an invalid. Or go crazy. She might even kill herself. Moriguchi acted so normal she didn't even seem sad. But that only served to make us realize how depressed she really was.

I was pretty sure Watanabe could tell that she was totally messed up, and that he'd be laughing to himself every time he saw her — and that made *me* laugh that much harder. At least that was how it was supposed to go.

Classes were pretty nice for a while. The teachers pretended to go on treating us as they always had, calling on everybody equally, but it was just a show. I'm not sure whether they didn't want to embarrass anybody or whether they just wanted to avoid any trouble in class, but for once they made sure to give the hardest problems to the smart kids.

Watanabe never had to struggle no matter how tough the question was, and when the teacher praised him, he pretended he didn't care. But now I could laugh at him when he acted all big like that.

You could see it on his face—*you think that stupid problem is going to stump me; I've done something much harder than that.* The stupid kid, he didn't even know he hadn't done it—but that I had.

The problems they gave to Watanabe even started to seem easier to me. We had a quiz on Chinese characters last week and I got all the hard readings. The teacher was impressed.

And why shouldn't he be? It might not happen for these next final exams, but before long I'd probably be getting better grades than Watanabe. When I realized that, the kids in class started to look totally dumb.

It was really hard not to laugh in their faces.

The kid tells his story in a trembling voice—one month after the incident. Moriguchi was coming to our house. I was already home when I got a call from her on my cell phone a little after noon on the last day of finals. She said she wanted to meet me at the pool to talk about something.

She knows, I thought. *That must be why she wants to meet at the pool.* My hand started to shake as I held the phone, and my heart was pounding. *Stay calm. Stay calm....*

Watanabe's the murderer. I was afraid I wouldn't be able to keep cool at the pool, so I asked her to come to our house. I decided to risk a question before hanging up.

"What about Watanabe?" I asked.

"I've just been speaking with him," she said, her voice all low and calm. I could feel myself relaxing. Everything was going to be okay. Watanabe was the murderer, and he had pulled me in against my will.

Moriguchi's sudden visit surprised my mother. I said I wanted her to stay with us while we talked. I was sure she'd want to know the whole story anyway, so it was better to have her there. I knew she'd believe me and try to help.

Moriguchi started with a really general question. "What sort of experience have you had at middle school?" she asked. This obviously had nothing to do with the accident, but I had decided I would tell the truth, no matter what she asked. So I told her about Tennis Club, and cram school, about my run-in with the high school kids at the game center, and how it felt when she didn't come to bail me out. I told her about being a victim but getting punished anyway—about every miserable thing that had happened.

She listened to all this, beginning to end, without saying a word. Then, just as I was taking a break to have a sip of tea, she asked her next question in this quiet, strangled voice that still seemed to echo through the living room.

"Naoki," she said. "What did you do to Manami?"

I put my cup down really slowly, but my mother practically screamed. She didn't know anything about it or whether I was involved, but she was already upset, and pretty mad. I knew I had to convince them that Watanabe had used me, that I was a victim, too.

So I told Moriguchi what had happened. From the time Watanabe had stopped me on the way home from school to the moment I was standing by the pool holding her daughter in my arms. I told her everything: the truth, down to the last detail. Watanabe had led me on and then double-crossed me. I never intended for anybody to get hurt. I told the truth, except for the very end. Just one little lie to wrap it up.

I was pretty sure my version would agree with what she'd heard from Watanabe. She hadn't interrupted me once the whole time I was talking, and even when I was done, she didn't say anything. She just stared down at the table and clutched her knees. But I could tell how mad she was. Poor, dumb lady. My mother didn't say anything, either.

We sat there for five minutes, and then Moriguchi finally turned to look at Mother.

"To be frank, as a mother, I feel as though I want to kill both your son and Watanabe. But I am also a teacher, and that leaves me with a dilemma. My duty as an adult and as a citizen is to report what the boys have done to the police, but my duty as a teacher is to protect my students. Since the police have ruled Manami's death an accident, however, I have decided to leave it at that. I will not be causing you trouble."

What? She wasn't going to the cops? My mother took a few seconds to take this in, but at last she bowed her head really low. "I don't know how to thank you," she said. I bowed, too. So, it was all going to work out.

We saw her to the door. The whole time she was there, she never once looked at me—I suppose because she was so mad—but I didn't really care.

Sitting at his desk, the kid looks really pale—one week after the teacher's visit.

The last day of the school year. After milk time, Moriguchi told us she was retiring. I have to admit, I was happy to hear it. I'd managed to get her to believe that Watanabe had killed her daughter, but I'd been nervous coming to school like this, wondering whether it would all come out and I'd be accused of being his accomplice.

"Are you quitting because of what happened?" Mizuki asked her.

I shot her a look, wondering why she had to bring it up, but Moriguchi didn't seem to mind. She started in on this long story, as though she'd been meaning all along to tell us what was on her mind.

She told us why she became a teacher in the first place. Then she talked about Sakuranomi-sensei and all the stuff he'd done. I didn't really care, I just wanted her to get finished and shut up.

Then she started talking about mutual trust between student and teacher and about getting texts—sometimes fake ones—from students asking her to come meet them or help them or something. She said the school had started a policy that when a call comes about a boy in a class where the teacher is a woman, they send the male teacher from another class, and vice versa. So that's why she didn't come when I got in trouble at the game center! It's a little late to be finding that out now.

She talked about being a single mother, then something about AIDS, and then about her daughter falling in the pool—and the whole time I felt like someone was tightening a noose around my neck.

"Mr. Shitamura happened to appear from somewhere...." Suddenly, she mentioned my name and I nearly choked, like the milk I'd just drunk was coming back up. She went on talking, and I was just managing to calm down when it came.

"Because Manami's death wasn't an accident. She was murdered by some of the students in this very class."

It was like somebody had pushed me into that cold, dirty pool. I couldn't breathe. I couldn't see. My arms and legs were flailing around, but there was nothing to hang on to.

Everything seemed to be going black, but somehow I knew it wasn't the time to be passing out. How much was she planning to say? I took a deep breath, trying to calm myself down.

That's when I was finally able to focus on what was going on in the room—and I realized that everybody was staring at Moriguchi. A minute ago they had all looked bored and were barely listening, but now they were all ears.

But instead of getting to the point, she launched into all this stuff about the Juvenile Law and that thing they call the Lunacy Incident. I had no idea what she was trying to say. She paused for a moment, and I was praying she might be finished, but then she went on, talking about her daughter's funeral. The next part was pretty surprising: She said that the girl's father was Sakuranomi-sensei, but that she'd decided not to marry him because he had AIDS.

I remember thinking that it was weird that Sakuranomi was going to die soon—because of AIDS—and being surprised that I could think about anything other than what was going to happen to me. I guess that was when I started rubbing my hands on my desk trying to make the feeling go away—the feeling that they were still holding the girl. If she had AIDS, then maybe I'd caught it, too.

We could hear chairs scraping on the floor in the next room. They must be done. Moriguchi seemed to have heard them, and I was hoping she'd let us go. And she did. She said anybody who wanted to could leave. My prayers were answered! But no one moved. If anyone—anyone at all—had gotten up, I could have sneaked out, but you could tell right away that no one was going to leave.

She looked at us for a minute, like she was making sure we weren't going anywhere, and then she started in again.

She said that she wasn't going to use names—that she was going to call the killers A and B. But that didn't mean anything, because as soon as she started talking about A, you could tell right away that it was Watanabe. I think she meant for everybody to know, to get them interested—and it worked: Everybody started turning around to look at him.

Then it was B's turn. The story was pretty much what I'd told her that day she came to the house. She'd sat there listening and not saying anything, but when she repeated back everything I'd said, she added these little comments that made me look stupid. Like I didn't do it because I was smart and wanted to prove something; I did it because I was dumb and couldn't do anything else. But what was the point of getting mad at her now. The game was over.

Now they were all looking at me. Some kids were

laughing, but some were shooting me looks like they really hated me.

I was going to get killed! I knew it.

It was all pretty simple: I went off to the game center—first bad move—and got punished; I was convinced my teacher was ignoring me; and so I became an accomplice to murder. Who wouldn't want to kill me? But it was really Watanabe's fault. I'm actually a victim. He's a murderer; I'm a victim. A = murderer; B = victim. A = murderer; B = victim. I repeated the formula over and over to myself.

Ogawa had another question for Moriguchi: "What if Wata...I mean, what if A kills somebody else?" he said. He seemed really into it.

"But you're mistaken. A didn't kill anyone in the first place," Moriguchi said. "It was B who killed Manami." I could feel myself being pulled down deep, to the bottom of the pool. She said the shock wasn't strong enough to kill; that Manami had only been unconscious.

They knew. She came to our house to find out, and now she knew. She still wasn't sure I'd done it on purpose, but that didn't matter anymore. It didn't change the fact that I'd killed her little girl.

Everybody was looking at me. I wondered what Watanabe was thinking, what kind of expression he had on his face, but I couldn't look. I was convinced the police would be coming soon to take me away. But then I realized Moriguchi was saying she wasn't going to trust the law to punish us. What did that mean?

Everything was getting dim around me. I'd fallen into

something, but not a pool. Some sort of thick swamp was swallowing me up, leaving only Moriguchi's quiet voice whispering in my ears.

"I added some blood to the cartons that went to A and B this morning," she was saying. "Not my blood—the blood of the most noble man I know, Manami's father, Saint Sakuranomi."

Sakuranomi-sensei's blood—AIDS blood—in the milk? The carton I'd drained to the last drop? I might be dumb, but even I could figure out what that meant.

Death. I was doing to die. Die die die die die die die die die die die die die die die die die die die die. I was going to die.

I could feel myself sinking deeper and deeper and deeper into the icy slime.

The kid staring out his bedroom window at the sky—just after the revenge.

Spring break. I spent my days in my room, staring out at the sky.

I wanted to climb out of the swamp and run away somewhere. Somewhere where nobody knows me. Somewhere where I could start all over from the beginning.

White jet streams stretch out all the way to the edge of the blue sky. I wonder how far they go. As I'm thinking about this, I remember something I heard once.

Weak people find even weaker people to be their victims. And the victimized often feel that they have only two choices: put up with the pain or end their suffering in death. But they're wrong.

The world you live in is much bigger than that. If the place in which you find yourself is too painful, I say you should be free to seek another, less painful place of refuge. There is no shame in seeking a safe place. I want you to believe that somewhere in this wide world there is a place for you, a safe haven.

Then I remembered who said it: It was Sakuranomi-sensei. I saw him on TV just a few months ago. Some joke— me remembering this now. He was so sure there was some-place I could go, but how was a middle school kid supposed to survive out in the world all by himself? Where would I sleep? What would I eat? Was anyone going to feed a run-away kid? Or give him a job? You couldn't last long out there without money. It was always the same thing: Adults gave you all this advice, but they could only understand the world on their own terms—they couldn't remember how it is to be a kid.

…When I was your age, I was always running away from home. My friends and I were always getting into trouble, and getting punished for it. But we never once thought about killing ourselves…. Why would we? When we had each other?

Maybe that's how it worked when he was a kid, but things are different now. Nobody really has any "friends"—I'm not even sure what that means. So if I'm going to go on liv-ing, I've got no choice but to do it in this house. My father works, my mother looks after me, and I stay right here. This is the only refuge I've got.

But what would happen if I give the HIV virus to my mother and father? And they get sick and die before I do. What would I do then?

I've *got* to make sure they don't get it.

That's my final goal as I live my last few days here in this swamp.

I seem to cry a lot in the swamp, but not because I'm sad. When I wake up in the morning and realize I'm still alive, the first thing I do is cry for joy. I pull open the curtains in my room and let the sunlight shine in, and though I know I don't have anything to do, I still cry at the start of a new day.

I cry because the food Mom makes me is so delicious. She fills the table with all my favorites, and I cry even harder when I realize I may not be around much longer to enjoy all this. I even tried those bean cakes I've always hated, thinking I should while I still had the chance, and I cried because I never imagined they would be that good. Why had I never given them a chance before?

They told me my sister's pregnant, and I cried to think about a new life coming into the world. Then I wanted to congratulate her in person because she's always been so good to me, but I couldn't risk infecting the baby, so I was left to cry all by myself.

But I'm not really unhappy. I don't really hate the way I am now. I thought it would be terrifying to live like this, knowing I was going to die soon, but my life is actually more peaceful than it was before.

I thought I wanted things to go on like this forever.

But then spring break ended.

I was entering eighth grade and I had to go to school. That's why they call it "compulsory education." I knew all that, but somehow I still couldn't make myself go. I'm a murderer. If I showed up at school, the kids in the class were going to punish me. They were going to hurt me. I was pretty sure they would eventually kill me. So how could I go?

But in addition to everything that might happen at school, I had another worry. I wasn't sure that my mother would let me stay home. I've been making up aches and pains every day since the start of school, but that can't work forever. Eventually she's going to get angry, or cry, or tell me how disappointed she is. I hate all of that, but it's not like I can tell her the real reason.

What would happen if she knew all the details about Moriguchi's daughter?

I threw her body in the pool after Watanabe killed her. That's what she thinks—and even that was a pretty bad shock. But how would she feel if she knew I had actually killed her, and that I had done it intentionally? Or that Moriguchi had taken her revenge by infecting me with the AIDS virus?

I'll tell you how she'd feel. She'd go completely crazy. But what would I do if she didn't want me here anymore? The thing I was most afraid of was being thrown out of the house. To me, that was the same as dying.

Then all of a sudden she came up to my room.

I was surprised that she didn't really push me to go to school. Instead, she wanted me to go see the doctor. She said I could stay home and take it easy for a while if they diagnosed me with a psychological problem.

Maybe I *was* sick.

But if I went to the doctor, they might find out about the HIV — and then my mother would know. That was a little scary, but I decided I could always run off if it looked like they were going to do any tests. Anyway, pretty much anything was better than being forced to go to school — where the kids were bound to kill me.

In the end, I shouldn't have worried so much. The doctor came up with a name for what ails me. It's called "autonomic ataxia" — whatever that is. But it turns out plenty of kids my age in Japan are staying home from school because they have it. My mother didn't seem particularly upset when she heard this. In fact, she seemed almost happy. At the very least, it meant that I could stay home and rest for a while, and that made me feel a little more relaxed, too.

When we left the clinic, I looked around like I was seeing the world with new eyes. I hadn't realized it that morning because I was so nervous, but this was the first time I'd been out of the house since that day. I was surprised to see that I could breathe the air out here like any normal person. Maybe I couldn't go to school, but I might be able to start going outside again.

I took a deep breath, like I was trying to check whether I really had come up out of the swamp, even a little bit — and that's when I caught sight of the Domino Burger by the station. It wasn't my favorite place — Watanabe and I hung out there during those few days when I thought we were friends — but when my mother asked me whether I wanted to get something to eat before we went home, I told her I could eat a hamburger. For one thing, I knew they used paper plates and plastic forks, so there was less chance of spreading the virus, but the real reason is that I needed to prove something to myself. I knew I wasn't ready to go back to Happy Town, but if I could face a place like Domino Burger, I thought I'd eventually be able to crawl out of the swamp.

I'd been so worried about dying that I'd completely forgotten about Watanabe—at least until I saw the Domino Burger sign. I suddenly wondered what he was doing. I was sure he must be locked away in his laboratory in that deserted house, worrying about dying too, and I have to admit the idea made me feel pretty good. He was getting just what he deserved—that's what I thought as I bit into my hamburger.

But just then something flew up all over my leg.

Milk! Milk! Milk!...They were sitting right next to us... Moriguchi and her daughter!

They were coming after me, pushing my head back down just when I'd been able to get it a little bit out of the swamp. Stop! Stop! Stop!...My head was going under the mud again. They were watching me, making sure I'd never get out. The slime was getting in my mouth, running down my throat.

I ran to the bathroom and threw up, trying to get the mud out. And the image of Watanabe along with it.

The kid peeks through his curtain and looks down at the vistors— about two months after the revenge.

I haven't been able to go outside again after the trip to the doctor, but I manage to get by here. It's nice and quiet. My room is the most peaceful, since I don't have to worry about spreading the virus when I'm in here.

I read manga on the Internet almost every day, and then I think up sequels to the stories and write those down in the notebook my mother bought me. I have to do a lot of cleaning, which is a pain, but it feels better than just messing around all day.

Then they showed up. Terada, the new homeroom teacher, and Mizuki. They said they'd brought copies of the class notes, and Mother let them in and talked with them in the living room. Which is right below my room. I could hear every word they said. Mother spent a lot of time telling Terada how terrible Moriguchi had been.

Then Terada told my mother she should leave all my problems to him. He said it in this really arrogant tone of voice, and I thought I was going to scream right through the floor.

Leave me alone!

I managed to keep quiet, but I started to feel really scared.

You could never trust teachers. This one was acting all nice and friendly, but he was just trying to lure me back to school so they could kill me. Terada had probably been Moriguchi's student or something. She was probably his guru. He acted like he was worried about me, but he was probably here to check up on us, see what we were doing so he could report back to Moriguchi. I couldn't even trust Mizuki. There was a rumor at school that she was Moriguchi's spy. Maybe Moriguchi still wasn't satisfied; maybe she had decided she wanted to kill me right away, and this was all part of her plan. My mother seemed to like Terada. What would I do if she let him come up here? He was probably coming to kill me. I just realized that Mother had been telling Terada all that bad stuff about Moriguchi. What if he went back and told her?

When Mother came up to my room looking all proud of herself, I screamed and threw a dictionary at her. Why did she have to go shooting her mouth off? She looked really shocked—probably because it was the first time I'd ever acted like that. As soon as the door was closed, I started to cry again. But I can't think of any other way to protect myself.

Terada and Mizuki come once a week, and every time I feel terrified. Mother doesn't let them into the house anymore, but she hasn't told them to stop coming. How much longer will this go on?

I've been afraid to go out of my room. What if somebody's outside? Moriguchi or Terada or Mizuki—or even that scary Tokura from the Tennis Club? I'm so frightened I can't do anything.

They all want to kill me.

If they find out I'm reading manga on the Internet, they'll kill me for that. I'm pretty sure Moriguchi knows which sites I'm going to almost before I get there. What if Terada left some sort of bug in the living room and Moriguchi's listening to every word I say? If she hears me saying something's delicious or I'm having fun doing something, she'll want to kill me even more.

They're watching me. And I can't do anything. I sit in my room and stare at the white walls, but the image of the pool and the little girl float up in front of me. I want to look away, but somehow I know I'm not allowed to.

Moriguchi has put a curse on me.

I spend the whole day staring at the wall. I don't know what time it is, what day it is. I can't taste food. I'm afraid of death, but I don't really feel like I'm living anymore. Maybe I'm not.

For the first time in days, I saw myself in the mirror. I looked miserable and filthy, but somehow I could see signs of life. My hair had grown. My fingernails were long. My skin was grimy. But I was still alive. I started to cry—I was bawling my eyes out.

I'm alive! Alive! Alive!

I had the proof—my long hair and fingernails, the grime on my skin. My hair covers my eyes and ears and hides my face; it protects me and lets me know I'm still alive.

The kid stares at the black mass—about four months after the revenge.

I woke from a deep sleep, as though I'd finally crawled out of some place I'd sunk into, and I found black things scattered around my pillow.

What was going on?

I shook my head to try to clear it and then picked up one of the black things, but it dissolved in my hand. Starting to panic, I put my hands to my head—and felt my ears.

That was my hair there on the bed. My hair! My hair! My life! Life! Life!

The mud at the bottom of the swamp began to dissolve and I began to sink again. The mud came oozing into my nose and ears. I can't breathe....

Death, death, death, death, death, death, death death

death death death death death death death death
death....

I don't want to die. I don't want to die. I don't want to die
I don't want to die I don't want to die I don't want to die I
don't want to die....

No! No! No! I'm afraid, afraid, afraid afraid afraid afraid
afraid....

Help me! Somebody!

But I was awake, and I was in my room, even if it had been
trashed somehow, and I was still breathing. I could still move
my arms and legs. I was alive. Or was I?

I left my room and went downstairs. Mother had fallen
asleep with her head down on her desk. This was my house
all right. I went into the bathroom and looked at myself in the
mirror.

Of course. I wasn't dead—how could I be if I still had
some hair?

I took the electric clippers out of the drawer. My mother
had cut my hair with them until I started going to middle
school. When I turned them on, they made a nice, quiet
buzzing sound. I put them up to my forehead, and a little
greasy clump fell at my feet—and with it, I could feel a little
part of me vanish. So that was it? The proof of life was the
fear of death. Then there was only one way for me to crawl
back out of this swamp....

Pressing harder, I ran the clippers over my head. With the
buzzing, I could feel strips of my life being peeled away.

When I was done with my hair, I cut my fingernails. Then
I took a shower and washed away all the dirt. I lathered the

soap into the washcloth and scrubbed over and over, and I could see the dirt falling off in flakes like the dust from an eraser. The proof of life went spinning down the drain.

So why was I still alive?

I couldn't understand. I'd scrubbed away every last shred of evidence—proof of my existence—and yet I was still breathing. Then I remembered a video I'd seen a few months ago.

Now I understood. I'd turned into a zombie. You could kill me again and again, but I didn't die. But it got better: My blood was actually a biological weapon. Maybe it would be fun to turn everyone else in town into zombies, too.

I decided to go out and touch everything on the shelf at the store—and thanks to the razor in my pocket, everything I touched would have a smear of sticky red blood.

Mission accomplished! The biological weapon has been detonated.

I went around and brushed my hand over every bento and rice ball and juice bottle like I was putting my stamp on them.

I wanted everybody to feel the same fear I did.

Somebody tapped me on the shoulder—a kid with bleached blond hair who probably worked here part-time. He's staring at my hand and he's got this really grossed-out look on his face. Blood's dripping from my palm where I cut it . . . drip, drip, drip, running nice and red . . .

It didn't really hurt before, but now that I'm staring at it I can feel it pulsing and throbbing. So I grab a box of bandages off the shelf and wrap it up.

My mother came to get me. She did a lot of bowing and

apologizing to the manager and the clerk. Then she bought all the stuff I got bloody.

The sun was still low in the sky as we walked home, but it was strong, like it was piercing right into me. As I walked along, squinting and wiping the sweat out of my eyes, I somehow stopped caring anymore about the fear of death or the proof of life. My hand was throbbing, and I was hungry.

And really, really tired. . . .

I looked over at my mother, who was walking next to me. She hadn't put on her makeup, and she was wearing the same clothes she had on last night. When she came to Parents' Day at school, she was always worried that she was older than the other moms, but that never bothered me. She was prettier than all of them. But this was the first time I'd ever seen her out without any makeup, and she couldn't even wipe away the drop of sweat running down her nose because she was holding the bags full of stuff I'd touched in the store. I had to squint hard to keep from crying.

I guess I've been misjudging her. I thought she wouldn't be able to love a kid who didn't live up to her expectations, her high ideals. But I was wrong. She's still here for me, even now that I'm a zombie.

I decided to tell her everything—and then get her to take me to the police. If she'd be waiting for me when I got out, I was pretty sure I could put up with my punishment. If she could accept me even though I'm a murderer, then maybe I'd be able to start over again.

But I didn't know how to say any of this to her. I knew I

should just tell the truth, but somehow I was still just a tiny bit scared she would give up on me if she knew.

But who am I kidding?

When it came right down to it, I just wanted to leave myself an escape route—which is why I decided to tell her what I'd done, but at the same time to keep pretending to be a zombie while I was telling her.

It was while I was explaining to her about what Moriguchi had done to me, about the AIDS milk, that I suddenly realized something really important: I didn't know whether I was infected or not. Or, if I was infected, whether I actually had the disease. What exactly had I been scared of all this time?

I could see the water in the swamp clearing up right in front of my eyes.

I suddenly felt free, and maybe that's why I could tell my mother that I'd killed Moriguchi's little girl—that I'd meant to do it. The way I'd felt that day by the pool—that feeling that I was better than Watanabe, better than anybody—came back to me as I was talking.

When I finished my confession, I could tell she was pretty shocked. I was hoping she'd agree that I needed to go turn myself in, but she just sat there. On the other hand, she didn't scream and push me away, either. She didn't give up on me, and that made me happier than just about anything.

But then she started asking me why I threw the girl in the pool even after she opened her eyes. "It was because you were frightened, wasn't it?" She must have said that ten times. I wanted to tell her it was because *I* was doing what Watanabe—the kind of kid she'd wanted all along—

couldn't do. *I* was succeeding where he had failed. But I couldn't say it.

I didn't want to upset her anymore, so I just kept telling her I was ready to go to the police.

They showed up again. Terada and Mizuki. But they don't scare me anymore. Let them come.

But then Terada started yelling outside the door. "Naoki! If you're in there, listen to me!" So I sat down next to my window to listen. At that point, I didn't care what he said.

"You're not the only one who had a hard time this term! Some of your classmates have been bullying Shūya! It's been pretty bad!" What? Watanabe has been going to school all this time? And he was still alive? Terada was saying that the kids had been punishing him, but they'd stopped.

I didn't listen after that. Instead, I remembered what Watanabe had told me by the pool.

We've never been friends. I can't stand kids like you anyway—completely worthless but full of yourself. Compared to a genius like me, you're pretty much a complete failure.

And I could just hear him laughing at me now, knowing I'm a *hikikomori*.

I had burrowed into my bed. The room was dark and I was grinding my teeth. I knew I was really angry, but I didn't know what to do about it. All this was Watanabe's fault, but he's been going to school like nothing happened. I felt like the world's biggest loser.

Even if Mother won't go with me, tomorrow I'm going to the police to confess. Everything. He may get off easier than me, but at least he'll know that I was the one who killed her—of my own free will. That'll get him. I'd like to see the look on his face when he finds out. I'd like to be there to have a good laugh.

I could hear somebody coming up the stairs. Must be my mother, and she must be coming to tell me she was ready to go to the police tomorrow. I was so happy, I went out to the hallway to wait for her. But....

As she got to the top of the steps I could see what she had in her hand. A kitchen knife.

What did she want?

"What are you doing?" I asked her. "Aren't we going to the police?"

"No, Naoki," she said. "That wouldn't change anything. That wouldn't bring back my sweet Naoki." She was crying hard.

"Are you going to kill me?"

"I want you to go with me, to see Grandma and Grandpa."

"You want to send me alone."

"No, I'm going, too."

She hugged me, and I realized for the first time that I was taller than she was. I suddenly felt really peaceful, and I knew it would be okay to die if she would come along with me.

Mother was the only one who ever understood.

"Naoki, my sweet boy. Forgive me. It's my fault you're this way. I'm sorry I wasn't a better mother. I'm sorry I failed you."

Sorry I failed you. Failed you. Failed. Failure! Fail, fail, fail, fail, fail fail fail fail fail fail....

She let go of me and rubbed my head. She had always been so good to me, petting me and spoiling me. There was a look of pity on her face.

"I'm sorry I failed you," she said.

Stop, stop, stop! I am *not* a failure! I did *not* fail!

Something hot splashed on my face.

Blood, blood, blood. Mother's blood. . . . Did I stab her?

Her body looked skinny and fragile as she fell down the stairs.

Mother, wait! Don't leave me! Mother! Mother! Mother!

. . . Take me with you.

That's where the images playing on the wall always end. But who's the stupid kid who keeps showing up here? And why do I know exactly what he's thinking?

And then there's that girl who says she's my sister. She was calling to me from outside the door.

"Naoki, you didn't do anything. It's all a bad dream," she said.

She called me "Naoki." I don't like being called by the same name as that idiot kid in the film on the wall. But if I actually am that kid, then the "bad dream" is that film itself.

And if that was a dream, what's this?

If only I could just wake up, have some of Mother's scrambled eggs with bacon, and go to school.

CHAPTER FIVE

The Believer

LAST WILL AND TESTAMENT

I know this is probably a creepy way to start an eighth grader's will, but happiness is as fragile and fleeting as a bubble of soap.

The one person I loved in the whole world died, and then that night when I got in the bath there was no more shampoo. Life is pretty much like that. But when I put a little water in the empty bottle and shook it, it filled up with these tiny bubbles.

That's when it hit me: That was me. Water down the last dregs of happiness and turn them into bubbles to fill the void. It may be nothing more than an illusion, but it was still better than the emptiness.

*　　*　　*

I planted a bomb at school today, the thirty-first of August.

It's rigged to go off when I push the Send button on my phone. I got another phone with a different number and built it into the bomb as the trigger. When it rings, the vibration sets off the blast. So actually you could set it off from any phone, if you knew the number—or even if you got a wrong number, you'd have about five seconds and then...KABOOM!

The bomb is under the podium on the stage in the gym.

There's an all-school assembly tomorrow to mark the end of the second term, and they're going to announce that an essay I wrote won top prize in a prefectural competition. My homeroom teacher, Terada, told me yesterday how the program was supposed to go.

I'll go up on the stage to receive a certificate, and then I'll go to the podium and read the essay. But they're in for a surprise. Instead of the essay, I'm going to give them some parting words and then detonate the bomb....

I'll be blown to tiny bits, and I'll take all those worthless idiots with me.

There's never been a child crime like this before, and I bet the TV and the newspapers will eat it up. I wonder what they'll say about me? I suppose they'll talk about my "inner demons" and use all the usual clichés; but even if the descriptions in the media are totally unrealistic, I hope this website, what I'm writing here, gets out just as it is. My one regret is that the newspapers won't use my real name because I'm a minor.

But I wonder what it is that the public really wants to know about a criminal. His background or his hidden psychological problems? Or maybe his motive for committing the crime? Well, if that's what they want, I'll start with that here.

I understand why murder is considered a crime. But I don't necessarily understand why it's evil per se. Human beings are just one among an infinite number of entities, living or otherwise, that exist on the earth. If obtaining some sort of benefit for one being necessitates the elimination of another, then so be it.

But that belief didn't prevent me from writing an essay on the meaning of life that was better than anyone else's in the class—better than any other middle school kid's in the prefecture. I began by quoting Dostoevsky's *Crime and Punishment:* "Extraordinary people have the right to violate conventional morals in order to bring something new into the world." But I argued against that idea, saying that life is precious and that under no circumstances could murder be justified. I even dumbed it down enough to sound like a middle school kid. The whole thing took less than a half hour to crank out.

But what's the point? That kind of conventional morality is nothing more than a lesson in school.

I suppose there are some people who have an instinctive aversion to murder. But in a country like Japan, where religion doesn't count for much, I suspect most people have been taught to value life above all else. And yet those same people also support the death penalty in the case of particularly brutal crimes—without seeing the inconsistency in their own position.

However, on a few rare occasions someone will come forward to counter this logic and argue that a murderer's life is just as valuable as one's own, regardless of status or station. But what kind of upbringing results in that sort of sensibility? I suppose it would come from a childhood where someone whispered fairy tales about the "precious value of life" in your ear every night before bed (if there are any such fairy tales). And if that were the case, I suppose I could understand ending up with that kind of attitude—even though it couldn't be further from my own feelings.

Because, you see, my own mother never once in my life told me a fairy tale. She did put me to bed at night, but instead of telling me stories, she talked about electrical engineering. Current, voltage, Ohm's Law, Kirchhoff's Law, Thevenin's Theorem, Norton's Theorem.... My dream was to become an inventor, to create a machine that did something new—extracted cancer cells, anything at all. That's how the stories my mother told always ended.

Our values are determined by the environment we grow up in; and we learn to judge other people based on a standard that's set for us by the first person we come in contact with—which in most cases is our mother. So, for example, a person who has been raised by a cruel mother might find another person—let's call him A—might find A to be a kind person; but another person who was raised by a very kind mother might find A to be cruel.

At any rate, my mother has always served as my basis for judging other people, and I have never yet met anyone who was as extraordinary as she is. Which means that I would have no regrets about the death of any of the other people around me. Unfortunately, that even includes my father. He's nice and cheerful—fine for the owner of a small-town electronics store—but that's about it. I don't hate him, but I don't think it matters whether he lives or dies.

Even the smartest person can go through a bad period in her life, a time when, through no fault of her own, she has the bad luck to be taken in by someone else. My mother was in the middle of such a period of weakness when she met my father.

She had been living overseas and came back to do a doctorate in electrical engineering at a top-ranked university, but she had run into a snag in her research just as it was reaching the final stages. Right around the same time, she was in an accident.

She was taking an overnight bus on her way home from a conference at our local university when the driver fell asleep at the wheel and crashed into an embankment. There were a dozen or so fatalities and many more injuries. My mother was thrown from the bus and suffered a major head contusion. She was loaded onto the first ambulance to arrive at the scene, and the patient on the other stretcher turned out to be my father. He had been on his way to the wedding of a college friend.

They were married soon afterward, and had me. Or perhaps it was the reverse. Having finished her doctoral studies, my mother abandoned her research, ignored her genius, and came here to live in this dead-end town.

You could think of the time she spent here as a form of rehabilitation. She spent her days in a corner of my father's electronics store—in a tired shopping district at the edge of town—finding ways to explain just a tiny bit of what she knew to her little boy. One day she might take the back off of an alarm clock; the next, she would take apart a TV—all the while telling me that there was no limit to the things that might be discovered in the future.

"You're a very smart boy, Shūya. I'm counting on you to accomplish the things I was never able to." She would often tell me this as she looked for ways to explain her abandoned research project to a child who was barely in elementary school—and perhaps she had a flash of inspiration while she was repeating the details. At any rate, she wrote a new academic paper without telling my father and submitted it to a conference in the United States. That was when I was nine years old.

Not long afterward, a professor from her old research lab came to persuade her to return to the university. I overhead their conversation from the next room, and I remember being so happy that someone who understood and valued my mother had come that I wasn't even particularly worried about her going away.

But she turned him down. She said she would have gone if she'd been single, but that she was a mother now and couldn't leave her child to go back to her research.

It was a shock to realize I was the reason she had to

refuse. I was holding her back. It wasn't just that I was a worthless kid; I was actually denying worth to the person I loved most.

When people talk about "overwhelming regret," it's usually just a figure of speech, but I believe that my mother experienced exactly that. All the feelings that she had suppressed came out, and they were directed solely at me.

"If it weren't for you," she would say as she began to beat me almost every day. She hardly needed an excuse—I hadn't eaten all my vegetables, I'd missed one problem on a test, I had slammed the door.... In the end, it was the very fact of my existence that she couldn't stand. But every time she hit me, I could feel a void opening wider and wider inside.

It never occurred to me to tell my father what she was doing. As I've said, I didn't hate him, but I had resigned myself to my mother's decision, and the longer I went on fooling him and pretending nothing was happening, the more I came to feel superior to him.

On the other hand, no matter how swollen my cheeks got or how many bruises I had on my arms and legs, I never felt any hatred for my mother. If she'd had a particularly violent outburst during the day, she would always come to my room at night and stroke my head while I pretended to be asleep. There were tears in her eyes as she whispered how sorry she was. How could I have hated her?

After she left my room, I would cry myself to sleep, my face pressed into the pillow to stifle my sobs. It was too painful to realize that the one person in the world I loved was suffering by the very fact of my existence.

It was during that period that I first started thinking about death.

If I were dead, my mother would be able to fully demonstrate her genius and finally fulfill her dream. Every suicide scenario I could think of began running through my head. Jumping in front of a truck out on the highway. Throwing myself off the roof of the elementary school. Stabbing myself in the heart. But all of them seemed ugly and unappealing. I remembered how my grandmother had died the year before at the hospital, almost as if she'd just gone to sleep, and I began to wish I could contract some disease.

While I was desperately trying to come up with a way to die, my parents finalized their divorce. I was ten years old. My father had at last realized that my mother was abusing me. It seemed that one of the other shop owners had told him. My mother put up no defense, saying she would move out as soon as the divorce came through. I understood that I couldn't go with her, but nevertheless I cried as if my body were being ripped apart, and when I was done, I was finally completely empty inside.

After my parents decided to divorce, my mother never hit me again. On the contrary, she took to gently stroking my cheek or forehead at random moments throughout the day. She made all my favorite foods—cabbage rolls, potatoes au gratin, rice omelettes—and her genius showed in the kitchen, too. Her versions were better than any restaurant's.

The day before she left, we went out together for the last time. She asked me where I wanted to go, but a flood of tears prevented me from answering. In the end, we went to a new shopping center called Happy Town that had just opened out by the highway.

She bought me several dozen books and the latest game player. She had me pick out all the games for the player I wanted, perhaps hoping that these would help me through the lonely days ahead. But she chose the books herself.

"These are probably a bit old for you now, but I want you to read them when you get to middle school. Each one of them had a big effect on me when I was growing up. With my blood flowing in your veins, I'm sure they'll be important for my Shūya, too." Dostoevsky, Turgenev, Camus...none of them looked very interesting at the time, but I didn't care. It was enough that I had her blood "flowing in my veins."

For our final dinner together, we ate hamburgers at a fast food place. She had suggested going to a nice restaurant, but I thought somewhere more starkly lit and unbearably loud might help me to keep me from crying.

We had a delivery service ship the things she'd bought and decided to walk home despite the distance. She held my hand in hers: the hand that could do such amazing work with a screwdriver, or make delicious hamburgers, or slap my face ruthlessly—and then pet me just as gently. I had never known until that moment how much could be communicated through the hands. But I had reached my limit. My tears flowed harder with every step we took, as I used my free hand to wipe them away.

"Shūya, you know I've had to promise that I won't come see you, or call, or even write to you. But I'll be thinking about you all the time. Even though we're going to be apart, you will still be my one and only child. If anything should happen to you, I'll forget about the promise and come running to find you. And Shūya, I'm hoping you won't forget about me...." She was crying, too.

"Will you really come?"

Instead of answering, she stopped and folded me in her arms. That was the last moment of happiness for her empty boy.

My father remarried the following year. I had turned eleven.

His new wife, someone he had known in middle school, was pretty enough but she was also impossibly dumb. Here she was marrying the owner of an electronics store, and she couldn't even tell the difference between AA and AAA batteries.

Still, I found I didn't really hate her. Mostly because she didn't pretend: She was fully aware how stupid she was. When she didn't know something, she just said so. If a customer asked her a difficult question, she would make a careful note of it and then ask my father before calling back with the answer. There was something admirable in this kind of stupidity. I took to calling her Miyuki-san, and the respect was genuine. I never once talked back to her or treated her like an evil stepmother, the way kids on those cheesy TV shows do. On the contrary, I was the model stepchild, finding a designer bag for her cheap on the Internet or going along with her to carry the grocery bags when she went shopping for dinner.

I didn't even mind when she showed up for Parents' Day at school. I hadn't mentioned it to her, but she must have heard from one of the other shopkeepers. Anyway, there she was, all dolled up and right in the middle of the front row. When I was at the blackboard solving some arithmetic problem that was too hard for the other kids, she took my picture with her phone, and then she showed it to my father when we got home—but I didn't mind. To be honest, it made me kind of happy.

Sometimes the three of us would go out bowling or to karaoke, and I began to realize that I was slowly becoming as stupid as they were—and that there was actually something unusually pleasant about being stupid. I had even begun to think that I could be happy being nothing more than a member of this family of dummies.

About six months after my father and she were married, Miyuki-san got pregnant. Since both the mother and father were dumb, it was pretty much a sure thing the child would be, too. Yet part of me was curious to see what kind of baby it would turn out to be—given that half the blood flowing in its veins would be related to me. By that point I had come to feel that I was nothing more than a happy member of this stupid family. But I soon realized that I was the only one who felt that way. About a month before the due date, on the morning that she had placed an order for a crib, Miyuki-san made an announcement.

"I've talked this over with your father, and we've decided to make a study room for you in your grandmother's house. It would be hard to concentrate on your schoolwork with the baby crying. Don't worry, we're getting you a TV and an air conditioner. You'll see, it'll be great."

It seemed that it had already been decided and that there

was no room for discussion. The next week, a van from the store picked up everything from my room and took it to the old house by the river. Before the end of the day, a brand-new crib had appeared in the sunny spot by the window in my old room.

I could hear the pop of a tiny bubble bursting.

Out here in the boondocks, there are no competitive schools. I was headed for our neighborhood middle school and had no need to study for entrance exams. As for the classes at elementary school—no matter what the subject, I could read the textbook through once to see what they were trying to teach us and then master the material in almost no time. I had no ambitions beyond that.

In other words, I had no need for a "study room." But there it was. So, in order to make good use of the space, and all this time I had on my hands, I decided to read the books my mother had bought me, even if I was starting a bit early.

I'm not sure what my mother got out of *Crime and Punishment* and *War and Peace,* but I felt that my own thoughts as I read must have been like hers, since the same blood ran through our veins. I loved all the books she had chosen, and read them over and over. As I read, I felt as though I were spending time with my mother, even though she was far away, and those were some of the few moments of happiness I had during those lonely times.

My study room had once been used as a storehouse for our shops, and as I sat in there, alone with the memories of my mother, I began to look around—and to discover what a treasure trove it was. I had nearly every electrician's tool imaginable, as well as broken or discarded electronics of all sorts. Among them, I found an old alarm clock, the same one my mother had taken apart to show me.

I replaced the batteries but it still didn't run, so I decided to try to fix it. Once I had the back off, I could see that the problem was nothing more than a faulty contact, but as I made the repair, I hit upon an idea. My first invention: the backward clock. I rewired the hour hand and the minute hand and even the second hand to run backward and give the illusion that time had reversed course. I set the clock to midnight, and from that moment on I began calling the study room my "laboratory."

I was pleased with the backward clock, but it didn't elicit much of a response from my audience—which consisted of the idiots in my class who brought me their porn videos hoping I would agree to override the mosaic effect on the nasty parts. They would stare at the clock without realizing that the hands were running backward, and when at last I was forced to tell them, they would simply shrug. "Oh, you're right," was the most I got out of them. One or two seemed a little more interested, but even these never thought to ask how I'd managed the reversal. Idiots like them believe that the world is limited to what they can see with their own eyes. They never try to figure out the inner working of things. That's why they're idiots—and why they're so completely boring.

When I showed it to my father, he simply asked whether it was broken. He was completely absorbed in doting over their new baby, which looked exactly like him—and was just as dull-witted.

My poor clock, my first invention, went completely un-appreciated. But what would my mother say if I showed it to her? She alone would be able to see its genius and praise my achievement. I could barely contain my excitement at the thought.

But how could I show it to her? I didn't know her address or telephone number. The only thing I did know was the name of the university where she was supposed to be work-ing. So I decided at that point that the best strategy would be to set up my own website, which I dubbed The Genius Professor's Laboratory. If I presented my inventions there, perhaps my mother would see them and leave a comment at some point. I knew the chances were slim, but that was what I was hoping when I entered my web address on the comments page of the university site and left a message:

> Brilliant elementary school student who loves electri-cal engineering presents his fascinating inventions. Please have a look!

But no matter how long I waited after that, there were never any comments that looked as though they might have been from my mother. The only visitors to the site were my idiot classmates, and when they mentioned that I could override the mosaic effect and uncensor porn, the number of hits from obvious perverts began to go up. Within three months, Genius Professor's Laboratory was nothing more than a hangout for twisted idiots. I tried posting some pic-tures of a dead dog I'd found down by the river, with the idea of scaring them off, but they seemed to love that even more, and the comments got weirder and weirder. Still, I never wanted to shut the site down, since that would have been cutting off my one chance of contacting my mother.

I continued working on my inventions after I started middle school. Our homeroom teacher for seventh grade turned out to be a female science teacher. I actually kind of liked her, particularly because she was a little aloof and never tried to be too familiar with her students. That sort of attitude is pretty rare with teachers these days.

I took her one of my new inventions, of which I was quite proud—my Shocking Coin Purse. How would she react? I was really anxious to see—but what I got was the hysterics of an old hag.

"Why would you want to invent something so dangerous? What were you planning to do with it? Kill small animals?"

One of my idiot classmates must have told her about my website, but she was an even bigger idiot to take the pictures of the dog seriously. Disappointing. That was the only way to describe it.

Right after this, however, I had a stroke of good luck, which came in the form of the National Middle School Science Fair. A poster announcing the competition appeared on the wall in the back of the classroom, with the names and titles of the six judges in small print. One was a science fiction writer, another a well-known politician, but what caught my eye was the name Yoshikazu Seguchi. Actually, I couldn't have cared less about the name—it was his title I noticed. He was listed as "Professor of Electrical Engineering in the College of Science and Technology at K University." The same K University where my mother was said to be working.

If I entered an invention in the science fair and this professor noticed it, word of it might reach my mother's ears. Would she be surprised to hear my name? Would she be happy to know that her son had won a prize using the knowledge she had bequeathed him? And would she be moved to offer a word of congratulations to her long-lost boy?

I was in a frenzy after that. I've always had the ability to focus when I need to, but I had never been so consumed by something in my life. First, I upgraded the coin purse by adding a release mechanism. But then I worked on the presentation values and the report, realizing that for a middle school project they probably looked at those even more carefully than they looked at the invention itself. Would they dismiss my purse as little more than a mechanized joke? Not if I could help it. I decided to bill it as a theft-prevention device. I made sure that the diagrams and the explanatory paragraphs were perfect, but I also crafted the "statement of purpose" and "project reflections" to sound like something a middle school student would write. I even wrote it all out by hand rather than printing it off my computer. The finished product was seventh grade science nerd perfection.

There was still one little problem: The application required a signature from the teacher who had served as your advisor, but Moriguchi had already told me what she thought of my purse. She must have been influenced by what she'd seen on my website, because she seemed shocked when I went to ask her to sign the form, but I had my line ready: "I can assure you I made this with the purest of motives, but you seem to think it's too dangerous. Why don't we let the experts decide which one of us is right?" In the end, she signed.

After that, everything went according to plan. Over summer break, the Shocking Coin Purse was entered in the local science fair in Nagoya and then went on to the national contest, where it was given honorable mention, the equivalent of third prize. I was a little disappointed at first, but in terms of my desired effect, third turned out to be even better than first: Judges were assigned to comment individually on each of the winning projects, and the judge for third place was none other than Professor Seguchi, the man from my mother's university.

"I take it you're Shūya Watanabe?" he said, coming up to me as I stood by my display. "This is quite an achievement. I don't think I could have built something like this myself. I've read your documentation, and I see you've applied a number of techniques you couldn't possibly have learned in middle school. Did your teacher help you with this?"

"No, my mother did," I told him.

"Your mother? You certainly are a lucky boy. Well, I look forward to seeing what you'll come up with in the future. Good luck."

He had used my full name and he absolutely had to know my mother. My fate was in this man's hands. I prayed that he would talk about what he'd seen today the next time he was with my mother. Or, if he didn't tell her, that he would at least leave the pamphlet listing the winners someplace she might find it.

After the meeting with the judges, I was interviewed by a reporter from our local paper. It was unlikely she would run across an article in a paper from a small town far from where she was living, but perhaps if she learned about the prize from Seguchi, she might go online and find the article. I could always hope.

The day I was interviewed, however, a seventh grade girl in some nowhere town committed a crime. The Lunacy Incident. She put several different kinds of poison in the food her family was eating and then blogged about the effects. I have to admit I was the tiniest bit impressed — once in a while one of these idiots comes up with an interesting idea.

I waited for the rest of summer break, but there was no word from my mother. Since she didn't know my cell number, I hung around the store all day and ran to the phone every time it rang. Miyuki was used to having me out of her hair since I'd been spending all my time at the laboratory and she didn't seem very pleased. I was constantly checking my email on the store computer, and I ran out to the mailbox at the slightest sound.

The TVs in the store played nonstop coverage of the Lunacy Incident. The girl's home environment, her behavior at school, her grades, the clubs she had belonged to, her hobbies, her favorite books and movies...if the TV was on, the details came pouring in.

Had my mother learned of the prize I'd won in the science fair in spite of all the Lunacy news? I found myself imagining her having coffee with Professor Seguchi in the university cafeteria.

"There was a kid at that science fair the other day...Shūya Watanabe, I think his name was...who came up with an interesting invention...."

But that's preposterous. Why would they be talking about me? They were probably discussing the whole Lunacy thing. As the coverage of that girl's idiotic crime grew more and more overwhelming, I had the feeling that bubbles were popping inside me. I'd done something wonderful and had my name printed in the newspaper, but my mother didn't know. But perhaps, just perhaps, if I did something horrible, my mother might come running to be with me again.

So that's it: my "early life" and my "hidden madness" and my "motive"—or at least the motive for my first crime.

Crimes, like anything else, come in all sizes and shapes. Shoplifting, theft, assault....But petty stuff like that gets you nothing more than a lecture from the police or a teacher, and if they wanted to blame anyone else, it would be my father or Miyuki. And what would be the point in that?

And I despise pointless things more than anything else in this world. If you're going to commit a crime, it ought to be something that can get people talking, whip the media into a frenzy—which means there's only one crime that will do, and that's murder. So I could steal a knife from the kitchen, run through the streets waving it around and screaming like a madman, and then stab the lady at the deli. That would get a lot of attention, no doubt, but when they went to find somebody to blame, again they would cite bad parenting from my father or Miyuki. What good would it do to have the newspapers writing about the influence those two had on my character development? What could be more humiliating than seeing my father on TV saying how sorry he was he'd sent me off to my study room instead of keeping me at home?

No, I had to get them to blame my mother. That was the only way to be sure she'd come to see me. When I'd done my deed, I needed to find a way to get the eyes of the world to turn toward her. But what did we have in common? Our genius, of course. So my crime had to somehow demonstrate the intelligence and ability I inherited from her...which meant it had to involve one of my inventions.

Should I come up with something new? Or was there something lying around that might work? Again, the answer was simple: the Shocking Coin Purse. Professor Seguchi had made the necessary connection himself at the award ceremony.

"Did your teacher help you with this?"

"No, my mother did," I had told him.

When a murder is committed, some of the attention naturally goes to the murder weapon. Knives or bats are boring. Even the Lunacy girl's potassium cyanide could be ordered online or stolen from school. In other words, the crime had relied on these tools without leaving room to demonstrate the murderer's own ability.

What would they say when they found out my weapon was something I'd invented myself? Not to mention that it had won a prize at the National Middle School Science Fair, the most wholesome place imaginable. That would get them talking. The judges who had awarded the prize would have some explaining to do, and at that point Seguchi might even mention that it was my mother who had inspired my technical wizardry.

But even if that whole scenario was unlikely, I was pretty sure my father would mention my mother's influence if he thought it would help him avoid responsibility for what I'd done. But I suppose I didn't have to worry about all this. I could always just make the connection myself. Tell them that instead of reading me fairy tales my mother had taught me electrical engineering from the time I was small.

I could imagine the outcry that would follow my confession. But what would my mother have to say? She'd tell me she was sorry, as she had all those times before, and then hold me in her arms. I was sure of it.

So now that I'd decided on the weapon, I just needed a victim. As a middle school student in a dead-end town, I didn't get around much. My spheres of activity were limited to: 1) home; 2) my laboratory; and 3) school. As I've said before, if I committed the murder at home or at my father's shop, the blame would fall on him rather than on my mother, even if it were committed with one of my inventions. I suppose I might have chosen one of the kids who played by the river near the lab, but in fact the place had a bad reputation and kids didn't come all that often, so it wouldn't be possible to plan things as carefully as I'd like. That left school. Which was fine, since murders at school always seem to get a lot of coverage in the media.

So, who should it be? The truth is, I didn't really care. I wasn't interested in the idiots and bumpkins in my class—I hardly knew their names—and I didn't think the media coverage would be much different whether I chose a student or a teacher. They'd go crazy for either one.

Middle school student kills teacher!

Middle school student kills classmate!

They both sounded pretty good...but also a little boring at the same time.

I was thinking about what made a person want to commit murder in the first place, what brought out the killer instinct—when I suddenly remembered the kid who sits next to me in class and scrawls "Die! Die! Die!" in his notebook. He's a pathetic piece of work, so worthless I'd been tempted to lean over and tell him he's the one who should die. But now it occurred to me to wonder who it was he wanted to kill. Maybe I should get him to pick my victim.

On the other hand, that wasn't the only reason I ended up talking to him in the first place. There was another element missing in my plan: a witness. What good was the murder if no one realized I'd done it? And yet, it would look too foolish to turn myself in. I needed someone who could follow me through the plan from beginning to end and then give a full account to the police or the media.

But not just anyone would do. First of all, I had to avoid anyone with a highly developed sense of morality. I also had to avoid anyone who might let the cat out of the bag while I was walking him through the plot. And, finally, I needed someone who wasn't categorically opposed to murder.

But there were other considerations besides. I had to avoid anyone who thought of himself as happier than me. Some kids, when they see someone worse off than they are, want to play therapist. "Why would you want to go and kill somebody? You must be unhappy about something. Why don't you tell me all about it?" What would I do if someone started that routine with me? The whole thing is just a trick—a way for them to make themselves feel better.

Fortunately, it wasn't hard to figure out the likely candidates. A week of observing my classmates gave me a good sense of who was who.

I had to avoid the complete idiots and the hangers-on seeking reflected glory. Then there were the idiots who had watched me decrypt their porn tapes but then went around acting like they could do it themselves. Or the would-be thugs who wanted to think of themselves as bad boys when the worst they'd ever done was visit my website and ogle the pictures of dead animals. I couldn't have the witness claiming he was actually my accomplice.

The ideal subject was an idiot—they were all idiots—who was harboring some deep resentment but was too timid to let it out. And Naoki Shitamura fit the bill exactly.

At the beginning of February I succeeded in increasing the charge in the Shocking Coin Purse. The time had come to put my plan into action.

I had never said more than two words to Shitamura, but as soon as I tapped him on the shoulder and buttered him up a bit, he opened right up. It was really quite simple. I mentioned the porn videos to him and the deal was sealed.

But almost immediately I began to regret having chosen

Shitamura as the witness. To begin with, I quickly figured out that he didn't have somebody he wanted to kill. He was just generally unhappy, and he scribbled "Die! Die! Die!" over and over because his limited vocabulary didn't afford him any other options to express his feelings. But beyond that he was simply depressing to be around. At school he was quiet enough, but give him an opening and he babbled on endlessly.

"Try one of these carrot cookies. Oh, I bet you're like me...can't stand carrots. I'm the same way. I won't touch them except in these cookies. My mom tried all these different recipes to get me to eat carrots, but they all sucked. But then she came up with these and they're really not bad...like I'm willing to eat them...for her sake."

I had no idea what he was talking about. It was a bit creepy for the mother of a middle school kid to send cookies along when her son went to play at another kid's house—which is why I hadn't touched them in the first place—but it was even creepier for the son to take them and not be totally embarrassed. It occurred to me that I should just kill him and be done with it. I did, however, have a useful realization in the midst of all this: Human beings have a fundamental need for physical and emotional space, and the desire to extinguish another life can arise when the boundaries of that space are violated.

But just as I was beginning to think about finding another witness, Shitamura mentioned a target that had never occurred to me: Moriguchi's little girl.

Middle school student kills teacher's daughter right at school!

That would be a first, and the TV and newspapers would eat it up. The homeroom teacher who had abused the boy when he showed her his invention. The same teacher who had signed the application to the science fair. Her little girl. Not bad—for an idiot like Shitamura. He even provided some additional information that could be of use: He had been shopping at the mall and had seen the girl begging Moriguchi for a pouch in the shape of a rabbit…which she had refused to buy her. I decided to keep Shitamura on as witness.

He got very excited about the plan, which he thought would end with the girl getting a little shock. He even started adding details—insisting, for instance, that someone needed to scout out the scene of the crime before we got started. The more I let him rattle on, the more eager he got.

"I wonder if she's going to cry?" he would say, with a revolting grin on his face. "What do you think? Will she?"

"I doubt it," I told him. Because she'll be dead. It was all I could do to keep from laughing myself sick at the sight of him making his little plans with no idea how they would end. Enjoy yourself while you can. You won't be grinning when you see her dead on the ground in front of you. He'd go running straight home, scared out of his mind, and tell his mother. That would be perfect. Especially since I remembered having heard that she was always complaining to someone about something. Apparently she wrote to the principal at the drop of a hat about any little slight to her boy. Well, I was going to give her something much bigger to worry about.

Everything was in place.

The afternoon in question, I got a text from Shitamura saying that he had done his reconnaissance, and I headed over to the pool.

He continued his annoying monologue while we hid in the locker room and waited for the girl. He would get his mother to bake a cake so we could celebrate, he said. What I didn't say was that I would never speak to him again once we were finished here, but the more he talked, the more I wanted to find a way to hurt him. But what could have been simpler? I just had to tell him the truth.

As I was enjoying imagining the near future, our victim arrived. She was four years old at the time, an intelligent-looking girl who bore a close resemblance to her mother. She looked warily about her but walked straight across the pool deck to the fence where the dog was waiting. Then she produced a piece of bread from under her sweatshirt and began feeding it to the dog piece by piece.

I had imagined a more pitiful child, given that she was the daughter of a single mother, but I realized immediately that I'd been wrong. Her pink sweatshirt was printed with her favorite rabbit character; her hair was neatly parted in the middle and held back on either side with bands decorated with pompoms. Her cheeks were soft and white. When she smiled at the dog, I felt as though I was looking at the fluffy rabbit thing come to life. She was obviously a well-loved child—at least to my eyes.

It's embarrassing to admit it, but at that moment I envied my victim. A little girl who should have been nothing more than a necessary piece—an object—in my plan.

But I managed to shrug off this humiliation and go out to meet her. Shitamura followed and then pushed past me.

"*Hi,*" he said as we got close to her. "You're Manami, aren't you? We're in your mother's class. You remember, I saw you the other day at Happy Town."

He'd jumped in and gotten things started. To be honest, I hadn't really thought he'd be any good at this stage of the game, but he actually was the first to speak up. He'd even thought up his line, and since his only real strength was his ability to seem friendly, this should have been a decent plan, but in the end it proved to be a disaster.

When he spoke to the girl, he sounded exactly like the third-rate MC they hired once a year for the block party in our neighborhood. He might have pulled it off if he'd used his normal voice, but instead he sounded like somebody pretending to be the nice boy from next door. The girl was eyeing him suspiciously now, and I knew I would have to do something or the whole plan would be ruined.

It was my turn to speak up. Shitamura could just watch from here on.

I asked her about the dog, and she got a big smile on her face. Humans truly are simple creatures. Then I watched for an opening and produced the pouch.

"It's a little early, but it's a Valentine's present from your mother." I hung it around her neck.

"From Momma?" she said, and I could see that she had the smile of someone who had been well loved—the smile I had lost forever.

That's when I realized I wanted her to die. I wanted to escape this humiliation, and the murder that would allow me to do it seemed even more precious. My plan suddenly appeared utterly perfect.

"Go ahead and open it," I told her. "There's chocolate inside." There was a look of complete trust in her eyes as she took hold of the zipper.

There was a quiet popping sound, her body twitched violently, and she fell over on her back. After that she lay perfectly still, with her eyes closed.

It had all happened so quickly that my bubble had no time to pop.

She was dead! My plan was a success. My mother would come now. She would take me in her arms and apologize for all the pain she'd caused me, and we'd never have to be apart again.

I was on the verge of tears, but Shitamura brought me back to reality. He was clinging to me and his body was trembling — which was totally disgusting.

"Go ahead, tell everybody all about it." Once I'd told him the most important thing, I shook him off and turned to leave.

I have nothing more to say to you, but your part begins now. This is the only reason I spoke to an idiot like you in the first place, why I took you to my laboratory and let you leave your nasty cookie crumbs all over.

But then I turned around. Shitamura was still standing there, a stunned look on his face.

"Oh, I almost forgot. Don't worry about them thinking you had anything to do with this. We've never been friends. I

can't stand kids like you anyway—completely worthless but
full of yourself. Compared to a genius like me, you're pretty
much a complete failure."

How well put! There was something refreshing about finally telling the truth. I turned again, and this time I left the
pool without looking back and went straight to the laboratory. Everything had gone according to plan.

I spent the night at the lab waiting for my phone to ring or
to hear the police on the intercom, but at dawn the next day
nothing had happened. Apparently Shitamura hadn't gone
sniveling to his mother yet—hardly surprising, as he was
slow at everything. But they must have found the body by
now.

There was nothing on the TV or the Internet, so I decided
to go by the house on the way to school to read the morning
paper. I had stopped eating breakfast there long ago, but
Miyuki said I should at least have a glass of milk. I drank
it down and then spread the newspaper on the dining room
table. On any other morning I would have started with the
front-page headlines, but this morning I went straight to the
local news.

Four-year-old girl drowns after sneaking into pool to feed dog.

Drowns? I went on to the article, certain there must have
been a mistake.

> Around 6:30 on the afternoon of the thir-
> teenth, the body of Manami Moriguchi (4 yr),
> daughter of Yūko Moriguchi, was discovered in
> the pool at S Municipal Middle School. The
> police are still investigating the cause of death,
> but it is believed to have been an accidental
> drowning.

Accidental? Worse still, there was no mention of electrocu-
tion. She had drowned.

What had happened? As I was trying to sort things out,
Miyuki let out a gasp.

"Why, this is your school, isn't it? And Yūko
Moriguchi...is your teacher! Her little girl died!"

As I write this now, I can see myself at that moment and
remember that I knew Miyuki was saying something important, but somehow nothing was getting through to me. It was
only slowly dawning on me that Shitamura must have done
something that made a mess of things. I hurried off to school
to find out what had really happened.

Up to that point I had thought that the word "failure"
had nothing to do with me or my life. I was supposed to
know how to avoid it, which mainly meant not getting involved with idiots. But I had completely forgotten this lesson
in choosing my witness.

School was buzzing with talk of the girl's death. The
body had been discovered by Hoshino, one of the boys in
our class, and he was telling anyone who would listen how
he'd found it floating in the pool. The pool had nothing to

do with it, I told myself. I wanted to tell those idiots that she was killed by Shūya Watanabe's prizewinning invention . . . so why didn't I?

The answer was simple. They didn't think it was a murder at all. Everyone was convinced it was an accident. The plan had been a massive failure. Not wanting to be seen as my accomplice, that coward Shitamura had thrown her in the pool to make it look as though she had drowned.

I was furious. But even more so when he showed up at school looking cool and calm, as though he hadn't done anything — hadn't ruined my plan.

I dragged him out to the hall and demanded an explanation.

"Leave me alone," he hissed. " 'We've never been friends,' remember? But you should know that I'm not going to tell anybody about yesterday. If you want to, go ahead."

That was when I realized he hadn't thrown the body in the pool because he was frightened; he'd done it expressly to spoil my plan.

But why? The answer was simple: to get back at me for what I'd said as I walked away. I'd underestimated him. A cornered rat will bite the cat, and there were idiots all over Japan doing unimaginable things simply because someone had pushed them too far. It was my own fault. I had given in to my emotions for one moment and provoked this idiot.

But in the end it didn't matter. I'd lost nothing. Nothing had changed. I could go back to being a model student for the time being while I worked on a new plan.

That ought to have been the end of it.

*   *   *

But it wasn't. The victim's mother, Moriguchi, found out the truth. About a month later, she called me to the science room and showed me the rabbit pouch, which was now dirty but intact. My wonderful invention, my murder weapon! I had succeeded after all! I wanted to shout for joy!

I confessed everything. I had wanted to kill someone with my invention, to attract even more attention than the Lunacy girl. But Shitamura, my witness, had lost his nerve and had thrown the body in the pool. I told her how sorry I was that no one had found out.

To be honest, I did everything I could to provoke her that day—so much so that I'm surprised, looking back on it, that she didn't kill me right on the spot. But I really didn't have much choice. It was my one chance to snatch victory from the jaws of defeat. But she just listened to the whole thing and then announced that she wasn't going to tell the police. She wasn't going to "give me the satisfaction of starring in my own horror show."

But why? Why? Why did all these idiots insist on getting in my way? Why all the recalcitrant pieces and parts?

Whatever the reason, she did as she'd said and kept quiet about the whole thing.

Then, on the last day of the school year, she announced that she was retiring from teaching, and as her parting message to us she began explaining exactly what had happened to her daughter. I wasn't sure why she was telling all those idiots when she hadn't said anything to the police, but at the very least it wasn't a boring good-bye. She overacted a bit in places, but on the whole it made a pretty gripping story.

As she got closer to revealing the identity of her daughter's killer, the other kids in the class started craning around to look at me. Their stares filled me with a deep feeling of satisfaction. There were worse ways of getting this started than having the rumor run through the school that I was a murderer. But then one of the idiots asked her why she hadn't gone to the authorities—whether she would feel responsible if A killed again. Her answer came as a shock.

"But you misunderstand when you worry about A killing 'again.'..." I knew every detail of the incident, but I have to admit at that moment I had no idea what she was saying. "The purse was incapable of stopping the heart of an old person with coronary disease, or even that of a four-year-old child."

She was saying that my invention hadn't worked, that Shitamura had killed the girl instead of me. I had simply rendered her unconscious; she had died when that idiot dropped her in the pool under the mistaken impression that he needed to cover up what we'd done. At that instant, every eye in the room turned toward Shitamura.

How utterly humiliating. Nothing could be worse. I wanted to bite off my tongue and die on the spot. But there was one more detail in Moriguchi's story—an especially interesting one: she had mixed the blood of an AIDS patient into the milk Shitamura and I had just drunk. If I'd been as much of an idiot as my partner in crime, I might have stood up from my desk and yelled, "Bravo!"

From the moment I first realized I was holding my mother back, I had contemplated suicide any number of times. But I'd been too young to come up with the right way to do it. I recalled praying over and over for exactly this: Please let me get sick.

Now I'd been granted my wish—in a most unexpected fashion. It was beyond anything I could have imagined, a complete success. If my mother would have come running to help a son accused of murder, she was even more likely to come for one who had AIDS. I was jumping for joy on the inside, as cliché as that might seem.

I wanted to run right to the doctor to get certification that I was HIV-positive and then send it off to the university where my mother was working, but I knew the virus could take three months to show up in my system, so I would have to wait to be tested.

As frustrating as it was, that was all I could do. In reality, however, I don't think I'd known such a peaceful period since my mother left. Under normal circumstances, my father would probably not have approved of my seeing my mother, but if I were ill, he would have no choice. I might even be allowed to live out my last days with her.

The incubation period for AIDS can be five or even ten years. We could develop a joint research project at her university. What kind of amazing things could the two of us do together? Then, when I was too sick to carry on with the research, she would nurse me on my deathbed.

As I played out this scenario in my head, vacation ended

and the new school year started. Shitamura didn't show up for class, and the rest of the idiots left me alone for fear of catching the virus, so all in all it was actually quite pleasant.

Gradually, however, the idiots began their little campaign of stupid pranks. They would shove milk cartons in my desk or shoe cupboard, or hide my gym clothes, or write "Die!" on my books. It wasn't fun, but I have to admit I was almost impressed by their determination and sense of invention in coming up with the would-be indignities. At one point, when a carton of sour milk exploded in my desk, I had a passing desire to slaughter the lot of them, but even that I could forgive—or at least ignore—when I realized it was just a matter of time before I would be with my mother.

When the three months had finally passed, I went to a clinic in the next town to have blood drawn for the test. Then, a week after that, I had a run-in with the class clowns. They're idiots, but even idiots can be dangerous in a group. As school was letting out, they grabbed me from behind and bound my hands and feet with tape. They had come prepared—with surgical masks and rubber gloves to avoid infection.

I thought they were going to kill me, and under other circumstances I might not have minded. But now I didn't want to die—not yet, anyway. Not when my dream was just about to come true.

If I started crying and asked for forgiveness, they might let me go. If I got down on my knees and begged, I might escape with my life. I was so determined to live that I would have put up with any humiliation. But as it turned out, I wasn't even the target that day. They were really after the class president, who was suspected of having squealed to Terada, the new home-room teacher. They had a special treat worked out for her.

When she insisted she was innocent, they told her to prove it by throwing a milk carton at me. It hit me in the face and exploded in a magnificent shower—but the shock reminded me of something completely different. I could feel my mother's hand on all those occasions when she slapped me. I don't know what kind of expression I had on my face, but at that moment my eyes met the president's—Mizuki's—and I saw her mouth the words "I'm sorry." Someone else must have seen her, too, because they declared her guilty and immediately passed sentence: a kiss. Apparently, that was why they had tied me up in the first place.

I had spent the walk home after this encounter wondering how there could be so many stupid human beings in the world, but those thoughts disappeared as I got to the door and saw an envelope from the clinic in the mailbox. At last! But the moment I ripped it open, I could feel myself tumbling into the abyss. It was negative. *I* was negative. I didn't have AIDS. I had known that was possible, so why had I been so sure I'd test positive? I suppose because Moriguchi had been so convincing that day.

I began to regret that the idiots hadn't just killed me earlier at school.

Late that evening, I sent a text to Mizuki asking her to meet me. I sent it because I had been unable to throw away the useless scrap of paper that had been waiting in the mailbox. It was useless to me, but it might be the difference between life and death for a girl who had been forced to kiss someone she was convinced had AIDS.

But to be honest, that was an afterthought. The truth is, I didn't want to be alone, and there was something about her that had interested me—if only slightly—before any of this happened. It had something to do with the fact that I had seen her at the pharmacy trying to buy some chemicals. They had refused to sell them to her, even though she said she wanted them for some dye work she was doing. I realized I could have made a bomb from the stuff she had wanted, and I wondered whether she might have had the same thing in mind.

Was there someone she wanted dead? If so, I even imagined we might hit it off. But when she showed up for my little meeting and I held out the results of my blood test, her reaction was a surprise.

"I knew," she said. But how could she have known my HIV status before I did myself? Maybe she meant she had read up on the transmission of the HIV virus and knew that the likelihood of infection from Moriguchi's little trick was extremely low. But when I took her to the laboratory and we sat down to talk, she had a completely different explanation.

Apparently, Moriguchi had never put the blood in the cartons in the first place. Mizuki had been the last one in the classroom the day Moriguchi told us her good-bye story, and she had found my empty carton and Shitamura's in the rack. She had taken them home and tested them with some chemicals she said she'd managed to get hold of. It seemed I had been under Moriguchi's spell the whole time. I'd been living in a fantasy of my own devising.

But why had Moriguchi gone to such trouble and told such a complicated lie? In the end, she hadn't turned us in or given us AIDS. What did her revenge amount to? Maybe she had only meant to torture us psychologically. If that were the case, I suppose you could say she'd hit a home run with Shitamura. I've forgotten to mention that he stabbed his mother to death and then went a little crazy. They say the police still haven't been able to question him. But Moriguchi couldn't have predicted that the day she gave her performance in front of the class.

The thing that surprises me, however, is that a momma's boy like Shitamura never told his mother he'd been infected with HIV. I'd have guessed he'd go right home and tell her, tears in his eyes, and then they'd have made daily trips to the clinic while they were waiting for the test results.

If Moriguchi was gambling on driving him crazy instead of actually killing him, she knew what she was up to. But what about me? I suppose it's true that Shitamura was the one who actually killed her daughter, but if I hadn't made the plan, she'd still be alive. I can't imagine she doesn't hate me just as much as Shitamura. Nor can I believe that she was smart enough to realize how disappointed I'd be that I'm *not* HIV-positive.

At any rate, whatever she was thinking, it was all a failure. A big bore, like everything else. It's boring to go on living, but just as boring to kill yourself.

I suddenly realized I needed some fun, a diversion of some sort. Maybe I should find a way to pay back all those idiots at school. First I needed to make sure they still believed I had AIDS.

The next day I staged a return engagement of the little drama they had scripted for the president and me the day before. It was all over in five minutes, and I found myself thanking Moriguchi for her parting gift to me.

So, you may be wondering at this point why I planted the bomb. I want to warn you against easy explanations, and you certainly shouldn't assume that it had anything to do with Mizuki becoming my girlfriend or that I was trying to compensate for my mother's love.

I hesitate to write about Mizuki here, but I will in order to avoid any inaccurate assumptions.

She is certainly bright enough, and she isn't silly like a lot of girls. There's nothing special about the way she looks, but there was nothing wrong with her, either. But none of that had anything to do with why I liked her. What I liked—even admired—about her was the fact that she stayed cool after Moriguchi's performance. While everybody else (and, I'm embarrassed to say, that included me) fell hook, line, and sinker for her crap, Mizuki showed the skeptical spirit of a scientist and tried to confirm those wild claims. But even when she found out the truth, she didn't go around telling everybody. She kept it to herself. That's why I liked her.

In fact, I liked her so much I was willing to stoop to pretty pathetic tactics to get her to like me back. "I just wanted someone to notice me," I told her. Of course, it wasn't "someone" I wanted. It was my mother. But still, the line seemed to work with Mizuki.

Unfortunately, she turned out to be a complete idiot. Or maybe it would be more accurate to say she was a fool.

During summer vacation, she would come to the lab every day, and while I worked on my new invention, she sat hunched over her laptop tapping out something on the keyboard. When I asked her what she was writing, she refused to tell me, and I let it go at that. I suppose she was my girlfriend at that point, but listening to someone else's little problems was still more trouble than it was worth. She finally told me that she'd been writing something to submit to a literary contest. That was a week ago today, the day she sent the whole thing off in the mail.

I told her I'd first noticed her when I realized she had those chemicals. I thought she might be interested in science, and that had made me want to get to know her. But as soon as she heard this, she began explaining the real reason she had them, as though she'd been waiting all along for the chance to tell me her secret.

She wasn't planning to make a bomb. But they weren't for some craft project, either. Nor was she planning to poison someone. Or kill herself.

She was simply obsessed with the Lunacy girl and what she'd done. When the news first broke, she had immediately been convinced that the girl was her other self. The name itself was proof enough, she said: *luna* meant "moon," as did *ʒuki*, the second character of her name.... She went on like this for a long time, but none of it made any sense. When I didn't say anything, she just kept talking.

She told me that there were other things that proved she

and the Lunacy girl were one and the same person. When they published the list of the chemicals the girl had in her possession in one of the weeklies, she had been speechless. They were exactly the same ones that she, Mizuki, had collected.

For what it's worth, that list had already been published when I spotted her trying to buy things at the pharmacy. It's hard to know whether she was telling the truth, but she said she used one of the chemicals she had on hand to test the milk cartons for traces of blood, so at least they turned out to be good for something.

At one point, out of the blue, she suggested testing some of her stock on Terada.

There was something gloomy about her, like a character in a bad after-school special (not that I've ever seen one), but I doubt she could have murdered anyone. Still, when the police questioned her about the incident with Shitamura and his mother, she blamed Terada for everything—and it seemed as though she still wasn't satisfied. But the whole thing struck me as a bit much. I could almost find myself sympathizing with the poor guy. He had been unlucky enough to take over from Moriguchi and then had let her prod him into the Shitamura debacle. But when I asked her why she had it in for Terada, her answer was unforgivable.

"I hate him because of what he did to Naoki. He was the first boy I ever loved...but I like you now, Shūya."

She was putting me on the same level as Shitamura. Could anything be more humiliating?

"Shit! How stupid can you be?" I had thought I'd said this

to myself, but apparently I said it aloud. Then, since it didn't matter anymore, I told her exactly what I thought of her obsession with the Lunacy thing. By that point she was furious, and she accused me of having a "mother complex."

I had told her a good bit of what I've written here, but it was wrong of her to describe it that way. Then when I tried to tell her that, she just pressed her point.

"I'm sure your mother loved you, but she made a hard choice in order to pursue her dream and she left you. She must have had her reasons, but in the end that's what it comes down to: You were left behind. But if you miss her that much, why don't you just go see her? Tokyo's not that far away, and you know where she works. The only reason you're still waiting for her is that you're a coward. You're afraid she'll send you away. You figured out long ago that she doesn't want you anymore."

That was too much. It wasn't just me she was attacking, it was my mother. The next thing I knew, I had my hands wrapped around her scrawny neck. At last I found myself truly wanting to kill someone—and there was no time to consider the weapon. There was nothing waiting on the other side of this murder. In other words, this was an end in itself, murder as its own reward. She died too quickly for me to hear the bubble pop.

Shitamura's experience had shown me that no one would pay much attention just because a minor committed murder. I decided her death was of no use to me, and I hid the body away in the laboratory's outsized refrigerator. But after a week, when no one came looking for her, I began to see how pitiful she was and thought I would take her with me the next day when I went to set off the bomb. After all, I had made it with her chemicals. She had brought them here to the lab because, she said, they seemed to "go with the place." In the end, though, I had to give up on the idea of carting her to school. Life may be as fragile and light as a bubble, but her body had turned into a lump of lead.

But again, I want to be perfectly clear. Planting the bomb has absolutely nothing to do with the fact that I killed the class president.

Three days ago I went to K University to see my mother.

All along I had wanted her to come to me. But as one of the conditions of the divorce settlement, she had promised not to contact me, and, being the serious person she was, the promise had kept her away all these years. Now I was taking matters into my own hands and making it possible for mother and son to meet again.

It took just four hours to get to the university—first on a local train, then the Shinkansen, and finally the subway. It had always seemed like another world, a paradise that could never be reached, but here I was after a short, easy trip. Still, as I got near my destination I could feel my chest tighten. I began to find it difficult to breathe.

Laboratory Number Three in the Electrical Engineering Department of the College of Science and Technology at K University. My mother's laboratory. As I crossed the enormous campus, my brain was running through various reunion scenarios.

I would knock on the door of the lab, and my mother would answer. What kind of look would she have on her face when she saw me? What would she say? She probably wouldn't say anything, just hug me tight. But what if one of her assistants or a student answered instead? I'd tell them I was here to see Professor Jun Yasaka. And then should I give my name? Or just wait for her to see me?

I was still trying to figure this out when I reached the Electrical Engineering Department and ran into someone I might have expected to meet here: Professor Seguchi, the judge from the science fair. Oddly enough, he seemed to remember me and spoke up first.

"This is a surprise," he said. "To what do we owe the pleasure?"

For some reason I couldn't bring myself to say that I'd come to see my mother, so I blurted out the first thing that came into my head.

"I had an errand nearby and I decided to come and see whether you might be here."

"Well, I'm delighted you did. So, have you brought along another invention?"

"I have," I told him. "Several, in fact." Nor was this a lie. I had brought the Shocking Purse and the Backward Clock and my Lie Detector to show my mother. Professor Seguchi smiled and led me off toward his lab, which was at the eastern end of the building on the third floor—and right under Mother's.

Once I had shown him the inventions, I could tell him I had actually come to see her.

He would say, You're Jun Yasaka's boy? No wonder you're so smart!

As all this was running through my head, we reached his lab and he showed me into a room that embodied all my fantasies—complex instruments crammed into every corner, shelves overflowing with books and technical journals. He sat me down on the couch and went to get me a cold drink. My eyes wandered around the room until they came to rest on a framed photograph on his desk. The picture showed Professor Seguchi and a woman standing in front of an old castle, perhaps in Germany. The woman next to the professor, who was smiling so happily, was clearly . . . my mother.

But what could this mean? Maybe it had been taken while they were at a conference together or on a research trip. Even after Professor Seguchi put the drink down on the table in front of me, I couldn't take my eyes off the picture.

He seemed to notice and laughed bashfully.

"I'm afraid to say it was taken on our honeymoon."

A bubble popped.

"Honeymoon?"

"I know, you might think I'm too old for that kind of thing. But we were married last autumn, and now at fifty I'm about to become a father for the first time. Strange, isn't it?"

"A father?"

"The baby's due at the end of December. But my wife doesn't seem to care—she's off at a conference in Fukuoka today. Women are like that now. . . ."

Bubbles popping, one after the other.

" . . . Your wife is Professor Jun Yasaka, isn't she?"

"Yes.... Do you know her?"

"She's...someone I greatly respect." I had started trembling, and that was all I could manage to say. The last bubble was gone. Seguchi was eyeing me suspiciously.

"You're not her...." I didn't wait around to hear the end of his sentence. I leapt up and ran out of the room. Though I never looked back, I was pretty sure the professor had made no move to follow me.

I thought she had given up on the idea of a family in exchange for the chance to follow her dream, to be true to her gift. To become a great inventor, she's been forced to abandon her beloved child.

Her "one and only child." Isn't that what she'd said? But she had never come back to find her "one and only." Instead she'd married up, found a better mate, had another child, and was living happily ever after.

It had been four years since she'd left me, but I'd finally realized the truth. It wasn't "a child" in the abstract that had held her back; it was me, Shūya, a boy with a name, and from the day she walked out of the house, I was already a thing of the past, already fading from memory. I was sure that Seguchi had realized who I was, so the fact that there was no word from her after my visit made this all too clear.

So you can think of the mass murder I'm about to commit as my revenge against my mother—and this last will and testament as the only way I have to tell her what I've done.

As with Moriguchi's daughter, I need a witness this time as well. So I've appointed you, the visitors to my website. I hope you'll be watching as I create a catastrophe that will go down in the annals of juvenile crime, and I hope you will tell my mother it was my way of showing her my pain.

Farewell!

Farewell!

I pounded on the podium as I finished reading "Life"—my stupid essay—and then reached into my pocket for my phone. The number was preset. I slowly pressed the Send button—that is, the detonator for my bomb.

One second passed, two, three, four, five....

...Nothing happened. What could have gone wrong? Was the bomb a dud? No, I hadn't even heard the vibration from the other phone I'd wired in as a trigger. It couldn't be? I bent over and peered under the podium.

The bomb was gone....

Someone must have seen the website and removed it. But who? It was a delicate business disarming a bomb. And why hadn't they called the police? Could it be...my mother?

Just then the phone in my hand started ringing. Number withheld.

My finger was trembling as I pressed Talk.

CHAPTER SIX

The Evangelist

Shūya? It's Momma....

Is that what you were expecting? I'm sorry to disappoint you, but it isn't Momma. This is Moriguchi. It's been a while, hasn't it?

I suppose you're wondering why the bomb didn't go off. Well, you see, I disarmed it this morning.

I have to say I was quite impressed with the mechanism. Clever of you to rig it so that the trigger was deactivated below a certain temperature. That way you could flash-freeze it at your little laboratory and bring it to school in a cooler. No matter how much it got shaken around, as long as it was cold it was safe enough. Your knowledge of chemistry is almost as impressive as your engineering skills.

If you had put that ability to good use, I'm sure you would

have made a wonderful scientist. But you chose to use your gifts for evil, to make weapons to carry out your stupid little schemes.

I read the love letter to your mother that you left online. Anyone who could write a thing like that and put it up on a website without dying of embarrassment must see himself as some kind of tragic hero.

It's a sad and beautiful story. Brilliant mother...her only son, blessed with the same genius. Tears in her eyes, she leaves the boy behind in the dead-end town to follow her dreams. But not without first promising him that she'll come running back if he should ever need her. The boy believes her. The father remarries, has a child with his new wife, and leaves the boy to a lonely existence. He wants to see his mother again, so he enters an invention in a contest. But there's no word from Mother. So he decides to kill somebody. Surely she'll come back if he finds himself in enough trouble, if he becomes a killer. Unfortunately, the plan is spoiled by a stupid classmate. Luckily, the victim takes revenge, and to his delight he finds out he's sick. Surely she'll come if he's ill. But it turns out he isn't—ill, that is. So he uses a girl, a classmate, to try to forget his troubles, but when she calls him a momma's boy, he kills her. Finally he decides to go visit his mother. But before he can see her, he meets her new husband and learns she's pregnant. It suddenly dawns on him that he is really and truly abandoned, and he decides to take revenge on his mother.

I know I skipped some of the details, but I think that's the general drift. And for the final act, you planted the bomb.

Are you a complete idiot? You use that word about everyone and everything in your love letter, but what do you think that makes you? What have you ever really created? What have you ever done for any of those people you looked down on? Any of your "idiots"?

You said you didn't think your own father deserved to live, but who do you think gave you life in the first place? Yet you seem incapable of understanding that fact, and you think that just because you get good grades in school you're some sort of anointed being. But you're wrong. You're the most deluded of all, the biggest idiot I've ever met.

That's the sort of person who killed my Manami, who snatched my precious girl from me. So I read your little postings and I decided to have my revenge, but I'm embarrassed to say that I've been a little vague. I should probably explain what I've been up to, beginning with my speech on the last day of school.

It's true that I collected blood from my husband, Sakuranomi, that morning while he was still asleep, and I brought it to school. The milk was delivered at nine o'clock and put in a refrigerator next to the office. I left in the middle of the assembly and used a syringe to inject some of the blood in the cartons destined for your cubby and Shitamura's. I even managed to find a spot on the crease where you wouldn't notice the tiny hole. Then, when you were done with the milk, I gave my speech. I knew how cruel your classmates could be, and I wanted to throw you to the wolves, so to speak. You see, adults are bound by rules and would protect you no matter how evil they knew you to be.

I never had any illusions about my chances of giving you AIDS. As you realized later, the transmission rate from a little joke like mine is extremely low. But as long as the chances aren't zero, I felt as though I had meted out a proper punishment.

And I thought I was finished with the whole thing. Not that my feelings had changed. I knew you would live with the fear of AIDS for a time and that your classmates would make you miserable, but that wasn't going to cheer me up. No form of revenge could have made me hate you any less. If I had cut the two of you to shreds with a knife, I think I would have hated the little pieces of you just the same. I realized that revenge was never going to wash away what had happened, never going to make me stop hating you with every ounce of my being.

Yet I believed I could force myself to put a stop to all this. I would never forget Manami, but I had no intention of spending the rest of my life dealing with children like you. My time with Sakuranomi was coming to an end, and when he was gone I intended to make a fresh start. I had never thought much about what I could do to help others, but I was determined to do so in my new life.

A month later, in April, when he knew he was dying, my husband told me something shocking. He said he was sorry he had never been able to make me happy, but he had at least wanted to be sure he wasn't leaving me behind to scandal and jail. So he had spoiled my revenge. He had felt me drawing his blood that morning and had realized I was planning something. He had followed me to school and seen me putting the blood in the cartons. Horrified, he had waited until I was gone and had replaced the cartons with new ones. He said he knew I might never forgive him, but that it was wrong to repay evil with evil, and that revenge would never make me feel any better. Even more importantly, he was convinced that you boys could be rehabilitated, made whole again, and he wanted me to believe it, too. He said I had to believe if I was ever to be whole again myself.

Those were his last words. That we should not seek revenge even though someone had murdered our child. That the children who had killed Manami could be rehabilitated. I suppose if anyone ever deserved to be called a saint, he did.

Which, according to your logic, would mean his mother must have been reading him fairy tales from the time he was a baby. But she wasn't. I doubt you ever bothered to look at the article about him that was posted in the back of the class, but his mother died soon after he was born. When his father remarried, he was in fifth grade—just as you were when your father remarried. Unlike you, he wasn't a model student and he couldn't get along with his stepmother, so he was constantly running away from home. His life after that was nothing to be proud of, and I'm sure he would have been on your list of idiots had you run into him along the way. And yet, a man like that wanted to save your life.

You may be right when you say that our sense of right and wrong is just something we pick up as children in school. Sakuranomi didn't learn many of those simple lessons until he was almost an adult, when he realized he had somehow missed out and felt he had to catch up, to make himself whole. You're like him in that, too—you somehow missed out on a basic sense of good and evil, and you even know it. But instead of trying to solve the problem, you act as though it's somehow cool to be bad, or you blame your mother for making you that way. Or perhaps you were afraid that by changing your behavior you would somehow be cutting ties with that absent mother—that bad girl you so much wanted to be like—so you refused to change. But none of that matters now.

I was never able to accept what Sakuranomi had done. I could never forgive him for insisting he was thinking about my happiness but acting like a teacher rather than a father until the very end. And it goes without saying that I can never forgive you boys, despite his desire to protect you. But revenge is a subtle thing, and I wasn't able to hit upon a new plan right away. So I decided to bide my time and see how things developed.

Werther-sensei, Yoshiteru Terada, has kept me informed about everything that has happened since I left the school. He was actually a student of Sakuranomi's, and since we overlapped a year, I remembered him quite clearly. He wasn't one of the more troubled boys in Sakuranomi's circle, but he did seem to idolize his teacher more than any of the others. So when he heard that his hero had tried cigarettes in middle school, he started smoking himself—though he mostly just coughed—and when the story went around that Sakuranomi had drawn graffiti on the car of a particularly cruel teacher, Werther tried that as well. Imitation was always getting him into trouble. But that meant he was unusually impressionable and thus quite useful for my purposes.

When Sakuranomi died, I was able to convince the media not to publish the time or place of his funeral. They seemed to buy the argument that such an admired teacher needed to "live on forever in the hearts of his students." But Terada managed to find out and came to the service. He said he needed to "make recompense for all the trouble he had caused his teacher," and while I was sick to death of platitudes, I could hardly turn him away. After the funeral, he knelt down in front of the memorial tablet and began apologizing for all his past offenses. I suspect that even Sakuranomi would have found the display distasteful, but I did learn something useful from his confession. He said that he felt it was his duty to carry on Sakuranomi's work, that he had decided to become a teacher, and that he had started work at S Middle School in April, at the beginning of the new school year.

I told him that I had taught at the same school until March, at the end of the previous year, and asked him how things were going. That was when he said he had taken over as homeroom teacher for the B Class. I suppose some things are just fated. He didn't seem to know I had been the homeroom teacher before him, so I asked about the class without telling him. He said his one problem was a student who had stopped coming to school. A boy named Shitamura. As I listened to Terada's account, I could tell that Shitamura believed he had contracted the virus but had not told his mother. It seemed a bit odd in this case, but I knew that there could be hidden walls between mothers and their children, and I began to think how I could make use of the situation.

In other words, I began to plan how I could drive Shita-mura even further into his own little corner. I offered Terada timely advice, always suggesting that it was what Sakura-nomi might have done in a similar situation. Sakuranomi would have gone to the boy's home, and he would have taken another student with him. At times Werther seemed a bit skeptical, but I knew that he would eventually come around and that when he did he would be utterly persistent. He would insist on going every week, and when he was turned away at the door, he would call up from the street. I could foresee everything.

I told him I would be happy to give him advice whenever he needed it, and that I would keep his confidences. And he must have felt that he couldn't discuss any of this with his colleagues at school, since he was constantly sending me email to ask my opinion. I don't think anyone should accuse him of being reckless in his dealings with Shitamura, since he was regularly in touch with the previous homeroom teacher.

He even wrote to ask me what to do when you were being bullied. He said he wanted to put a stop to it, but I told him that rather than doing it himself, it would be more effective to have one of the other students confront the bullies. That way the class could identify the problem as a group. I had been hoping to intensify the attacks against you, but in the end the situation got twisted around, as so much with Terada always does, and poor Kitahara-san suffered the brunt of their cru-elty. This is one thing I truly regret.

I suppose if she hadn't been caught up in all this, you would never have killed her, and I am terribly sorry, but whenever I feel guilty I am immediately reminded that you boys are ultimately to blame. None of this is my fault. You killed Kitahara-san. She hit too close to home with the words "mother complex," and you murdered her in a blind fury. What did you call it? "Murder as its own reward"? What does that mean? The word games of an idiot.

While I was just sitting back and watching the two of you, Shitamura killed his mother. I can't imagine what happened between them, and even if I could, I wouldn't pretend to understand. But the one thing I can say with certainty is that Shitamura would never have killed his mother if he hadn't killed Manami in the first place. So in the end I have no sympathy whatsoever for the boy or his mother. In her case, it was her reward for raising him the way she did. Despite Sakuranomi's interference, I felt that my revenge against Shitamura was complete.

Which just left you. As you've said yourself, while it was Shitamura who actually killed Manami, she wouldn't have died had it not been for your stupid plan. I wanted to see you both suffer and die, but if I were forced to decide which of you I hated more, it would be you.

I would have been perfectly content had your classmates killed you during their brutal games, but my hopes were dashed when Terada reported that he had "solved" the bullying problem. He seemed so happy with himself, and he thanked me for the advice I'd given him. He was amazed that the threat of infection had actually turned out to be useful in keeping the other children at bay—something he might have realized from the beginning.

Be that as it may, I could see now that I would have to take matters into my own hands. Still, I was quite certain that you would never feel sorry for what you'd done to Manami even as the life was being choked out of you. So what was the point? I needed to find your weakness. Though it seemed futile, I checked your website daily. But there were no postings after the news about your theft-prevention purse. Still, the lack of updates was a clue in itself: Since I knew you despised useless things, why had you not shut down the site? I had all but given up on a speedy revenge and resigned myself to watching and waiting. If it took forever, I would discover something you loved and then destroy it. But just at that point, you returned to your site.

Thanks to your love letter to Momma, I was able to learn a good bit about your unhappy childhood. I even began to think that things might—and I emphasize *might*—have turned out differently had I been more supportive when you brought me your purse. I almost felt sorry for what I'd said. Almost. Fortunately, I came to my senses and realized that was all a lot of nonsense. You said it yourself: The wallet was meant as a trap. You wanted to shock someone; that's why you made it. Why should I have been supportive of that? The notion that you wanted my attention and praise is just the delusion of a spoiled child. What you wanted was the chance to show off. You ignored the opportunity to make something worthwhile and chose instead to create a useless toy to impress people. Who would find that praiseworthy? You should have been content to play with the purse yourself.

You refuse to see value in any human being except your

mother, and you'll have to live with the person that has made you. You can't blame your crimes on someone else; they're your own responsibility. But if fault is to found elsewhere, the only other person to blame would be your mother, a woman who raised her hand against a child who couldn't meet her expectations, who denied that child a place in her heart, and who ran off to fulfill her own dreams, leaving behind a boy with an unrequited love. In that sense, in your tremendous egotism, you and your mother truly are alike.

So you planted the bomb to take revenge on your mother. You were going to get back at her by killing lots of innocent people. It was the same with Manami. You have no feelings for anyone but your mother, yet you hurt everyone except her.

If there's no one else in your little world but you and your mother, then I encourage you to kill her and leave the rest of us alone. But you won't. You're too much of a coward. Which is why I can't allow you to go on talking big and hurting innocent people.

The police will be arriving at school soon, and they'll find Kitahara-san's body before long. Once you've been arrested and they make the connection between you and Shitamura, the truth about Manami's death will come out. Still, I worry the punishment you receive may not be sufficient. Then too, a bright boy like you will be able to convince them you've reformed, and you might soon be back in society, your past expunged, ready to embark on a glittering future.

But before all that, I have just one more thing to tell you.

After I read your love letter and disarmed the bomb, I

went to see someone. I suppose I was feeling a certain amount of sympathy for you, and it could be that I wanted one more chance to think about what Sakuranomi had told me. You might even say that I realized that some part of the responsibility for Manami's death lay with me.

At any rate, I went looking for the person you have been longing to see for all these years—and it turned out to be the simplest thing to find her. First, I showed her your website, your sweet love letter. Then I told her about Shitamura and what the two of you had done to Manami.

Do you want to know what she said?

Sorry, I couldn't make that out. It's a bit noisy. Can you hear the sirens and all the shouting?

You see, I didn't just disarm your bomb, I reset it somewhere else. Then I prayed you wouldn't press the switch to detonate it. But of course you did. It wasn't a dud, you know. I'm not sure how big an explosion you thought you would cause, but I can tell you it was impressive—enough to blow away the better part of a reinforced concrete building. Fortunately, I had every faith in your ability and was waiting at a safe distance. Otherwise, I wouldn't be here to make this call.

The bomb went off in Laboratory Three in the Electrical Engineering Department at K University. Your bomb, detonated by your own hand.

Funny—I think I've finally had my fill of revenge now. And with luck, I've at last started you out on the road to your own recovery.

About the Author

Kanae Minato is a former home economics teacher and housewife who wrote *Confessions*, her first novel, between household chores. The book has sold more than three million copies in Japan, where it won several literary awards, including the Radio Drama Award, the Detective Novel Prize for New Writers, and the National Booksellers' Award, and was adapted into an Oscar short-listed film directed by Tetsuya Nakashima. Minato lives in Japan.

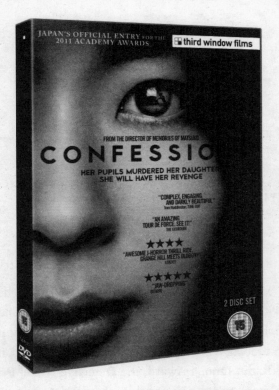

If you enjoyed the novel, you might like to know
that it's been adapted into an award-winning motion
picture from director Tetsuya Nakashima.

Confessions was shortlisted for Best Foreign Language
Film at the 2011 Academy Awards.

'Please, whatever you do, watch *Confession*s.
I thought it was breathtaking.'
Claudia Winkleman

Now available from Third Window Films